Mystery in Arles

MABEL ESTHER ALLAN

Mystery in Arles

NEW YORK
THE VANGUARD PRESS, INC.

Contents

CHAPTER ONE

A Holiday in the Sun

IT ALL STARTED on the day I left school forever, though, as I sat high on Primrose Hill, I
hadn't the faintest idea that I would soon be going
to Provence. I was in an utterly depressed and restless
mood, too upset and unsettled to go home. So I sat
there on the short grass – dry for once, though we had
had seemingly endless rain until a few days before –
and stared down at London, the buildings dimmed
by smoke and a slight haze.

I had always loved Primrose Hill and all my life I
had sought refuge there when I was miserable or
wanted to think. As it was a fine day there were plenty
of people around me, but I scarcely noticed them. I
was still fighting angry disappointment and wondering, with the utmost gloom, what I could do now with
the ruined weeks that lay ahead.

'I do feel awful about it, Damaris,' Nancy had said,
when she met me that morning outside the school's
main entrance. She had just poured out the news that
we could not go wandering in Northern France after
all. 'We've all looked forward to it so much and saved
and saved. But Ronald can't help it. He just has to
start that new job now, instead of in three weeks'
time, as he thought. I tried to convince Mother that
we could go alone and that we'd be quite all right.

After all, I'm eighteen and you'll be eighteen in two months' time. But she won't hear of it and now it looks as though Robin and I will be going to stay with our aunt in Cumberland.'

Oh, we had made so many wonderful plans, and, as Nancy had said, we had saved for months for that holiday in France. Our parents had agreed because Nancy's brother Ronald was twenty-two and had done a good deal of travelling in Europe. With Nancy's younger brother, Robin, who was sixteen and a nice, lively boy, we would have been a party of four and we had planned to wander just where we pleased, starting in Rouen and using local buses and sometimes just our feet. There had been endless studying of maps and we had hoped to go from Normandy into Brittany.

France had always attracted me strongly since I was quite a small child, perhaps because my cousin Celia had some French blood through her mother. Celia, nearly four years older than I, had been going off to France to visit relatives since she was about eleven and I had always loved to listen to her occasional stories of the romantic house in Provence where she had spent so many happy holidays. I had been to Paris with the school and that was all, but my French was good and I had always planned to go again just as soon as I was old enough to argue that I'd be all right on my own. Parents can be so fussy and it's dreadfully hard to convince them that one has common sense and can look after oneself.

Anyway, I had spent that last day at school sunk in utter gloom, and the gloom had very little to do with the fact that I would never again be a schoolgirl. I didn't mind leaving school; I felt I had had quite enough of it. My last year had been spent studying mainly languages and commercial subjects, and the plan was that I should have a few months at a good business college and then look around for an office job. I am one of those people with few real talents; perhaps an ability to learn languages is the best of those I have. I love acting and am not bad at it – I took the lead three years running in the school play, always an ambitious affair – but I knew perfectly well that I must always remain an amateur. I hadn't the quality that would bring success in the hard world of the professional theatre.

So there I sat on Primrose Hill on that July afternoon, with no real future of any kind. The only immediate possibility – and one that didn't please me much – was that I might join my father and mother and the children at the cottage in Devon they had rented for three weeks. In fact I should probably *have* to join them unless I could think up another feasible plan very quickly. They would never agree to leaving me alone in the house.

The pangs of hunger made me move at last. After all, I couldn't sit there forever, miserably thinking about that lost holiday in Normandy and Brittany. So I walked slowly away to the nearest gates and five minutes later I was in the quiet road where we had lived since I was a baby.

When I let myself in with my key Mother was in the hall, arranging some tall gladioli in a big white vase. She took one look at me and demanded:

'What's the matter, Maris? Are you so sad about leaving school?'

'Not sad about that,' I said, and sitting on the bottom stair, with my shabby school case at my feet, I poured out the story of the disappointment. Mother was immediately very sympathetic.

'Oh, that is hard luck. I'm terribly sorry. I know how you've looked forward to it. We must cancel your ticket, then, and we shall just have to squeeze up in the cottage to make room for you. The children will be pleased.' Then she seemed to realize that my face didn't register unalloyed delight, for she went on: 'Devonshire sounds dull after France, I know, but it really does seem to be a charming spot and very near the sea. You can go bathing there.'

I nodded and went slowly up the stairs to my own room. My sisters, Dorcas and Ruth, aged nine and eleven, shared the one next door, and a good deal of cheerful chatter reached me through the closed door. I hoped they hadn't heard me and shut my own door softly. Then I gave a disgusted groan as I caught sight of myself in the looking glass. I looked grubby and unglamorous in my blue school dress, with a shiny nose and my dark hair looking as though it hadn't been brushed for a week.

'Damaris Cleveland, I hate the sight of you!' I said to myself.

Well, a bit of glamour might cheer me up, and thank goodness I had finished with a school uniform for always.

I felt much better after a bath, and I put on a pretty pink dress, sheer stockings and high-heeled shoes. With my hair well brushed and some make-up on I felt a lot more human and adult. I was nearly ready and had already been called three times (we always had a kind of high tea about six o'clock in term-time), when the doorbell rang. I opened my bed-room door a little and heard Celia's high, clear voice.

'It seemed such an age since I'd seen you all, Auntie. I did telephone from school during break this afternoon, but no reply. So I thought I'd just come and hope there was enough food for me.'

My cousin Celia was a teacher in a Primary School and that day marked the end of her first year.

'Of course there's enough,' Mother said cheerfully. 'Maris, aren't you ever coming down?'

'This minute!' I shouted back, thankful that I had taken the trouble to remove all traces of the grubby schoolgirl. I went downstairs and found everyone except my father sitting round the big table in the dining room.

'Phew!' cried Ruth when she saw me. 'Are you going somewhere special?'

'Nowhere,' I said. 'I just hated the look of me when I came in and thought I'd better do some-thing about it. Hullo, Celia!'

We are all dark, but Celia is darker, looking more as though she has Spanish blood than French. She must have just come from a gruelling last day of term, but she looked quite fresh and very charming, not at all like a teacher, though some of them can be quite attractive.

She grinned at me.

'Hullo, Damaris. So you've put it behind you at last?'

'But the poor girl's just had a dreadful disappointment,' Mother said, and went on to explain how we could not now go to France.

'That's too bad,' said Celia, sounding very sympathetic.

'I believe it was you who started her on this passion for all things French. She's always envied you that French blood. You're not going to Provence this summer, are you?'

Celia nodded.

'I am now, as a matter of fact. I was going to stay at home for the first three weeks of my holiday and re-decorate the flat all through, but— Well, I've changed my mind. I'm off to Arles next Thursday.'

'It's a big house, isn't it?' asked Mother, and Celia answered yes, it was quite large. I guessed what was coming, and maybe Celia did too, but she didn't look very forthcoming.

'Couldn't you take Maris with you, Celia? The Gironelles sound so nice and she really wouldn't be any trouble. She speaks good French and she'd be thrilled to see all those wonderful Roman remains in Provence. I *know* she thinks she'd be bored in Devon.'

For years I had had a secret dream that Celia would take me with her to Arles, but it had never before been put into plain words. The Gironelles were, of course, not related to us, and, though Celia had always seemed to regard them as her second family, she had never so far as I knew taken any of her English friends there, let alone thought of taking a young cousin. I had always suspected that she liked to lead two quite separate lives, and, in any case, I had never seen very much of Celia, though I had always admired her. A gap of nearly four years can seem large when one is young.

'I – I don't really think I could,' said Celia, looking very embarrassed. I wished that Mother would not pursue the point, but she went on, quite as though she had not noticed anything unwilling in Celia's manner.

'We should be so grateful if you could. There really *won't* be much room at the cottage and we couldn't leave Maris here alone, even if she does consider herself grown up now. Couldn't you just *ask* the Gironelles? We'd be glad to pay for a long telegram, and of course if they say no, then that's that.'

I felt simply dreadful, because I could see that Celia didn't like the idea. It was obviously cheek even to ask her, and I wished that Mother were more sensitive to atmosphere. Sometimes she could be very dense. But I was hurt as well, because I really would have adored to go and Celia had always seemed to like me.

My father came home soon after that and Mother at once told him about my disappointment, adding:

'Celia's going to Provence next week and I've asked her if she can take Maris with her.'

'Well, that would be a pleasant solution,' Father said slowly, glancing from me to Celia. 'But Celia can hardly take an uninvited guest.'

'But the Gironelles must have heard all about us

long ago and Celia has always said how hospitable
they are, loving visitors. Why she once said that M.
Gironelle asked a couple of English boys to stay just
because he met them on a train and liked them. So
I—'

'Let it go,' I muttered. I was feeling thoroughly
miserable again by then. But Celia suddenly said
quite cheerfully:

'All right, I'll send that telegram. I'd *like* you to
come, Damaris, only—' She did not finish the
sentence.

'I'll telephone you and let you know,' she said,
when she left soon after the meal.

The result was that I was to go to Arles with Celia.
I answered the telephone myself the next day and
when I heard the news my heart leaped with a
mixture of pleasure and dismay. I longed to travel
south to that land of hot sunshine, bleached stone
and ancient history, but if Celia didn't want me—

'You only need bring thin clothes,' Celia was saying. 'And perhaps one or two sweaters and a thin
raincoat. It can be chilly when the mistral blows, but
you won't need a heavy top coat. I'm spending a
night in Paris and going on by the fast morning
train. O.K.?'

'Yes,' I said. 'Thank you, Celia.' And then:
'Look! I feel awful about it. Mother just forced me
on to you. But I really won't be much trouble. I shall
like exploring on my own.'

There was a slight pause and then Celia said
quickly:

'You've got it all wrong, Damaris. I always meant
to take you to Provence one day. When I was there
at Easter I even discussed it with the Gironelles and
they said they'd love to meet you. Then I promised
to go to Scotland around the 20th of August, and the
flat really does look a wreck, so I thought I wouldn't
go south until Christmas. You were going to France,
anyway – or so I thought then. It's just— Well,
there's a special reason for my going now. Maybe I'll
tell you later. Not that I know much myself.'

'Oh, I see.' I felt much better, not quite such an
interloper. 'That sounds mysterious.'

'It is, rather. It worries me. Anyhow, stop feeling
that I don't want you. It may be quite a good idea for
you to be there, too. Oh, and don't worry. I've fixed
up about your tickets and reservations. I changed my
seats and got two together on each train. That was
lucky, wasn't it, at the very height of the holiday
season? My travel agent is quite a pal of mine.'

'Father said he'd send you a cheque if you fixed
it up.'

'Right. Be at Victoria about nine o'clock next
Thursday morning, under the train indicator.
There's sure to be a mob travelling. We'll have an
evening in Paris and perhaps visit our favourite
haunts.'

'I love Montmartre.'

'So do I, though not so much in August. I like the
Butte when there are no crowds. Good-bye, Damaris.
Be seeing you.' And the line went dead.

So I was going to the ancient town of Arles. I was
going to see that sun-soaked land that was already

familiar from the pictures of Cézanne and Van Gogh. Van Gogh had lived and painted in Arles and had shown to the world that countryside of cypresses, cornfields and vineyards. Orchards too, lovely in the spring, and pale stones under a burning blue sky.

I felt a great deal better after that talk with Celia, for I thought she meant what she had said. But – something was taking her to Provence when she had not meant to go again until Christmas. Something, presumably, to do with her beloved 'second family'. I couldn't imagine what it was and didn't really try. I thought she would probably let me into the mystery, whatever it was.

I rushed upstairs – I was alone in the house – and began to root through my clothes. In Normandy I would not have needed anything very attractive (we had planned to carry rucksacks and nothing else), but the Gironelles were quite well off and they might entertain a good deal. I had two pretty sun-dresses, luckily, scarcely worn during that dreary summer, a green nylon dress that would be lovely on hot southern evenings, and a few fairly new cottons.

I sang loudly as I sorted through my underwear, for now I felt a different girl.

CHAPTER TWO

Celia Explains

I STILL KEPT a faint feeling of uneasiness and vague hurt, for it went against the grain to be foisted on someone, and one side of me resented it very much. At a time when I wanted to feel wholly adult it shook my self-confidence, I suppose. I certainly made up my mind that Celia wouldn't find me too much in the way. I was more than prepared to explore on my own, and with this in view, I went to my favourite map shop in Long Acre and bought several Michelin maps of Provence, abandoning the Normandy and Brittany ones for another occasion.

That same day Father came home carrying a parcel and tossed it to me.

'A present, Maris. Thought it would be useful.'

It was a Blue Guide to southern France and had cost over two pounds. I was very thrilled with it, for it had everything, including street maps of Arles, Avignon and other places. I do love history and find ancient history particularly fascinating, and the thought of all those wonderful remains – Roman arenas and theatres and the great aqueduct called the Pont du Gard – fascinated me. The place names sounded very exciting: Avignon, Nîmes, Tarascon, Orange. I sang 'Sur le Pont d'Avignon' so much that the children caught it too, and in the end Mother protested that she never wanted to hear it again.

'But she's going there!' Ruth cried enviously. 'Avignon isn't far from Arles. Maris showed me on the map. So she really will stand *"sur le Pont"*. And they have bullfights in those huge Roman arenas – someone gave us a talk about France last term. Will you go to a bullfight, Maris?'

'I hope not,' I said, shuddering. 'Not unless the Gironelles arrange it and I can't get out of it.'

'But Celia's been to several. They're not supposed to *kill* the bulls in France.'

Yes, I remembered Celia talking about it once and I'd thought how strange it was that someone who loved animals could lend herself to anything so barbaric. But Celia had some Provençal blood and perhaps it made a difference. The very thought of the heat and the crowds and the tormented bull made me feel very grimly Northern. I made a mental note, however, not to say so in front of the Gironelles.

I got a book about the Camargue out of the library: that strange country of saltings and reeds and rice fields that is very close to Arles on the west. On the Camargue they breed black bulls and white horses and, reading about it for almost the first time, it sounded remote and very fascinating. I vowed that I would go there as soon as possible, to look for flamingoes and all the other birds. I little thought then that part of the adventure would be played out in that wild area under a burning summer sky, with the mistral harshly stirring the reeds that were far taller than I.

I was so caught up with thoughts of the romance of Provence that it was not until the day before I was due to leave that I thought much about the Gironelles. For, in fact, it was *people* who would concern me before scenery and birds and I had never before lived in a foreign household.

I began to feel horribly nervous about the Gironelles. My French really was quite good, and I had been pleased to find that I could manage fairly well in Paris, if people didn't actually gabble. But it would be quite a different matter to have meals with a French family every day . . . to have to try and be intelligent. I hadn't the faintest idea if they spoke any English; it was something Celia had never mentioned. She had been bilingual since she was a child, so presumably it had never seemed important to her.

I knew a little about the Gironelles. Apart from Monsieur and Madame there were two sons, Valérien and Paul. Valérien was about twenty-five and owned a bookshop in Arles, and Paul was younger, about twenty-three. I thought he was something to do with law; maybe he worked in a solicitor's office. Mother had sometimes said that she wouldn't be surprised if Celia married one of them, but Celia herself had never mentioned such a possibility. They were not first cousins, only second, and it would probably be just the thing for Celia if only she were to fall in love with one of them. And, of course, if one of them were to fall in love with her.

I also knew something about the house in Arles. It was called La Vieille Maison – The Old House – but once its name had been Le Prieuré and it really was very ancient, built round several courtyards. Celia had once said it was the most enchanting house she had ever seen.

By evening I had boiled up into quite a state of excitement and nervousness, but I was far too proud to let my family realize it. My cases were packed and everything was ready.

'You've got your passport?' Mother asked. 'And your French francs and travellers' cheques?'

'Everything, thanks,' I assured her. Father was paying my fare, which was far more expensive than it would have been to Normandy, but a good deal of the rest of the money was my own, saved from last Christmas and my weekly pocket money. I'd also had a temporary office job in the Easter holidays. It gave me a nice feeling to think I wasn't entirely dependent on my long-suffering family. When you are nearly eighteen you begin to think it's time you were earning and not having other people pay for your pleasures.

After that afternoon when I sat so dismally on Primrose Hill the weather had turned awful, and it was raining when I went by taxi to Victoria to meet Celia. A faint mist wreathed the heavily green trees in the parks, and cars were splashing along. It seemed almost unbelievable that by the next afternoon I would be in Provençal sunshine.

For travelling I was wearing a light-weight green suit, and just then I had a sweater under it and my nylon raincoat on top. It was cold. . . . *I* was cold, probably partly with excitement and nervousness.

But I felt much better when I found myself under the indicator at Victoria Station and I was very, very much aware that I was lucky. I was going to the South of France instead of to Devonshire, where it would probably be too cold to bathe.

There were plenty of other lucky people in the world too, by the look of things, for the crowds were enormous. Ten past nine came and I began to grow nervous again, wondering if Celia would ever find me in the crush. I was entirely hemmed in by a huge party and every member of it wore a badge. They seemed to be going to Naples and they were very excited. One woman from Lancashire had lost her luggage, and another her dearest friend, or so I gathered from her agonized wails.

Then I saw Celia. She looked cool and calm and very smart and she was followed by a porter carrying two cream suitcases. She edged round the Lancashire woman, who promptly stood on her delicately shod foot, and, grimacing, turned to me.

'Hullo, Damaris! So you made it? Heavens! What a mob! How I hate travelling at this time of year. I'd have flown to Marseilles, but even my travel agent friend couldn't get me seats.'

'It's rather fun, though,' I said, and then hoped that I didn't sound hopelessly young and inexperienced.

Celia said, 'I hope you still think so by the time we reach Arles!' and we walked towards the barrier.

The train was already crowded, but we found our booked seats near the front and Celia settled herself placidly with a couple of glossy magazines on her lap.

I had a Penguin book, but I didn't feel like reading while so much of interest was going on, so I sat watching the flurried, harassed-looking people going past the windows.

Then the whistle blew and we were off, moving away slowly over the Thames and then through the outskirts of London, grey and depressing in the heavy summer rain.

'Oh, well,' said Celia, looking up from her magazine, 'maybe it's a good thing we're going south. I must say I'm glad now.'

The train gathered speed and went rocking and roaring towards Dover, and I sat dreamily, occasionally turning from the window to look at my cousin. I began to wonder why, in fact, she had not intended going to Provence until the mysterious emergency arose. She *always* went to Arles – Christmas, Easter and summer. Her parents were dead and she had a small private income as well as her salary, so I suppose it helped to pay the high fares. The flat might need redecorating, but it wasn't like Celia to stay away voluntarily from her beloved France.

Looking at her covertly, I suddenly realized that she seemed rather tense, in spite of the surface appearance of great calm. The hand lying in her lap was clenched; I could see the bones pressing against the rather thin white skin. There was something tense about her cheek bones too, and I didn't think she was really reading. She had not turned a page for quite a while. I thought that human beings are very shut away and you can never be really sure what is going on in their minds. I wondered if Celia would talk to me . . . tell me something about whatever it was that was so worrying, but she went on staring at the magazine and I turned back to the soaking cornfields and orchards of Kent.

Then there was the Channel, grey in the rain, but looking reassuringly calm, and we began to struggle into our raincoats and collect our things.

The steamer was absolutely jammed with people, but we managed to get seats in the bar and Celia ordered sandwiches and fruit drinks, saying we'd have our main meal when we reached Paris. Paris! My heart leaped with pleasure, for I had loved it the previous year.

After we had eaten we went and stood on the deck in the rain, with hoods over our hair, and Celia chattered quite gaily, commenting most amusingly on the people. But she said nothing about herself or the Gironelles.

The French train was also crowded and there certainly wasn't a chance of private conversation. The rain had stopped as we approached Calais and the sun was shining brilliantly as we sped through that vast country of spreading cornfields and chalky ridges. Coloured awnings were out in the little towns that we passed through, and already the dismal greyness of London seemed far away.

It is so beautiful, that country that lies on the way to Paris. Woods and farms and orchards and little lanes and woodland rides that simply ask to be explored. It was not really so very far from where we might have started our tour, if Ronald had not had to let us down. I even wished for a while that I was not going to an alien household and a countryside that would certainly be alien too. The thought of the Gironelles still frightened me a little.

In Paris Celia always stayed at a small hotel on the Left Bank, not far from the Sorbonne. We took a taxi from the Gare du Nord because we had rather too much to carry to go by Métro, and after we had unpacked a few things and washed, we went out for a meal at a restaurant in the Boulevard St Michel. It was wonderful to sit at a table on the pavement, protected by a little blue fence and some shrubs, and to eat French food again. I was so happy that I ceased to worry about Celia or the Gironelles, and I ate a hearty meal. It was exciting to hear French spoken on every hand and to watch the passing people. To be in Paris . . . not as a schoolgirl, much protected, but as a young woman. A passing young man – very handsome – winked at me and then leaned over a shrub to say: 'Mademoiselle is English? Mademoiselle is very pretty!'

Oh, yes, definitely no longer a schoolgirl!

'I'll have to watch you,' said Celia, grinning. 'Come to think of it, I don't know much about you, Damaris. How many boy friends have you had to date?'

I felt myself blushing, she looked so sophisticated and amused.

'Oh, a few. No one who's – really mattered.'

'What about that Ronald who was conducting you and the others to Normandy?'

'Oh, he's nice. But I've known him for ten years;

as long as I've known Nancy. I'm not in love with Ronald.'

She continued to talk lightly while we drank our coffee and she smoked a cigarette, but as we rose and walked towards the Seine she grew rather silent and, glancing sideways at her, I saw that her brow was a trifle creased.

I was aware of Celia at my side, but I was, just then, ten times more aware of Paris. It grows dark earlier in Paris than in London and it was already sunset as we crossed the Pont St Michel and came to the Ile de la Cité. In the west the sky glowed a brilliant rose, shading to a clear apple green. The buildings were beginning to stand out blackly – the Préfecture, the Palais de Justice, with the delicate spire of Sainte Chapelle just showing, and the towers of Notre Dame.

The island was crowded with strolling people, there was music in the distance, and the River Seine gleamed below us – that same river that I might have seen at Rouen. But then I should not have visited Paris again and breathed its magical atmosphere. Presently we leaned on a parapet and stared down at the water and I distinctly heard Celia sigh. So then it seemed time to try and establish some understanding between us.

'I think you'd better tell me,' I said slowly. 'Why are you worried? Why are you going to Arles when you didn't mean to? I'm not a schoolgirl now. I'll understand.'

Celia looked at me, but it was some moments before she spoke.

'There isn't much I can tell you, as I said on the telephone. I had a very personal reason for *not* going this summer. But Tante Lucille wrote to me and begged me to come. She didn't understand why I had decided not to come in the first place. She wants me to come because she thinks I may be able to get something out of Paul. He's worrying them all dreadfully. Apparently he hasn't been himself almost since I was last there, in April. He's such a gay person, as a rule, but he's been morose and strange, going off by himself and seeming desperately troubled about something. He's obviously short of money, too. Tante Lucille said she knows it sounds unlikely – what can Paul ever have done to invite it? – but they wonder if he's being blackmailed. But he holds them off, he just won't discuss his affairs at all. And – and Paul likes me. I can probably get it out of him.'

'Oh!' It all sounded rather alarming; the word 'blackmail' had a very ugly ring. 'Is he – in love with you?'

She nodded, looking very sombre.

'I'm afraid so. I did even wonder, at first, if it could simply be that; that he was upset and missing me. But it wouldn't account for the shortage of money, and really Paul isn't the kind to take unrequited love *that* much to heart. Things were growing very difficult between us, though. That was partly why I decided not to go this summer.'

'You don't love him?'

'No,' she said, frowning fiercely at a Bateau Mouche that was slipping towards us from under the nearest bridge. People were waving, but she did not wave back. 'Oh, well, all right. No, you're *not* a schoolgirl. I've always liked you, Damaris. But it goes against the grain to admit, even to someone one likes, that one is in love with a man who doesn't seem remotely aware of it.'

'Valérien,' I said, though actually it could have been anyone she had met during her many visits to Provence.

'Yes. I've been in love with him for two – no, three years. Paul was always my friend when we were younger. Valérien is older and he was always a little remote. He's rather a studious type. Very bookish and he's published a few short stories and literary articles. There isn't anyone else, as far as I know; he just doesn't seem very interested in women. And I suppose he just thinks of me as a relative who's always been around. At Easter, with Paul following me everywhere and Valérien being perfectly charming but as remote as the moon, I felt I'd had enough. I never *thought* I'd be such a fool as to love someone like this. I've tried to forget him. I've talked to myself by the hour. And now— Well, I'm such a complete fool that I can't wait to see Val again.'

Well, just then I was far more interested in the love story part of it than in Paul's troubles, strange as they sounded. My heart went out to Celia, whom I had always thought so gay and happy.

'You hid it very well.'

'I don't wear my heart on my sleeve,' she said bitterly. 'I 'as me pride, ducks. But that's how it is. And my main job is going to be to try and get some sense out of Paul, though I mustn't rush it.'

We strolled on then and presently stood on the Pont Neuf, looking down on the gardens that make a little tip to the Ile de la Cité. Young men and girls went past us, laughing, and the sunset was dying behind the distant Eiffel Tower. Celia suddenly said abruptly:

'I'm tired. Do you mind if we go back to the hotel and go to bed? I'm not being a very lively Paris companion, I'm afraid.'

I agreed and we strolled back up the Boulevard St Michel, looking at the shops. Celia talked of other things, lightly, and the Gironelles were not mentioned again until we were parting outside our rooms. Then she took a photograph from her bag and held it out to me.

'Valérien and Paul.'

Celia was in the picture too, standing between the two young men. I could easily tell which was Valérien and which Paul, for one certainly looked older, far more mature and perhaps not quite so good-looking. They were both dark, with regular features, and both wore open-necked shirts and looked equally sun-tanned. But there the resemblance definitely ended, for Paul was laughing and looked ten times more alive.

'He looks as though he could never be worried about anything,' I remarked, privately much astonished that she should prefer the older brother.

'Paul? Well, he does take his work seriously nowadays and he has plenty of brains. But he always has laughed a lot. Even when – when I rejected him he didn't treat it as heavy tragedy, though

I think he does love me as much as he ever will anyone. I feel awful about Paul, but there's nothing I can do on that score. As for this other thing – I just can't imagine him apparently worried to death.'

I couldn't either. As I got ready for bed I found myself remembering that handsome, laughing face. Paul Gironelle! It seemed strange that I was going to meet him the very next day.

In the morning we went to the Gare de Lyon and boarded the southern express. It was going all the way to Italy, through Marseilles and Nice. But we would leave it at Avignon, where Celia had told me we would be met by car.

It was quite a cool morning, but sunny, and there were even more people travelling than on the previous day. It was an enormously fast train and very noisy and once again we didn't talk much. I read a little, tried to listen to the French conversation around us, and sometimes gazed out at the swiftly passing scene. It was beautiful, with woods and farms and hills, but not really thrilling until we reached Lyons and then there was the River Rhône, which we would follow all the way. We had lunch in the restaurant car – a real French lunch, with wine – and when at last we returned to our compartment the countryside was changing. The sky was blue all over, with not the faintest sign of a cloud, and everything looked dustier and more golden.

Most of the buildings seemed to be of stone, shading from pale cream to a warm ochre, and a great deal of the corn had been cut. There were rows of vines, not terraced as I had expected, and orchards laden with fruit. It looked a bleached land, pale under the blazing sun, and by then, to me, everything was beginning to seem dreamlike. I was tired, hot and rather untidy, and I could scarcely believe that soon I would set foot in Avignon.

'I wonder who'll come to meet us?' said Celia, as the train began to slow down. Avignon looked huge and this part was quite modern, with factories and great blocks of flats. It was a shock, as I had been expecting a medieval town.

'Who might?' I asked, knowing that she was terribly keyed up.

'Well, not Paul or Valérien. They'll both be working. It might be Oncle Jean or maybe Gaston – he's a kind of handyman. Oh, I expect it'll be Oncle Jean. He's half retired now, though I believe he still goes into Marseilles two or three times a week.'

We stepped out into heat that seemed to have actual substance, but I scarcely had time to notice it. I was sufficiently occupied in trying to keep Celia in sight, for the crowds kept surging between us. It was a big station and it took us some time to reach the exit. Beyond there were trees, parked cars and taxis, and, not far away, a great pale gateway and the soaring bastions and ramparts. So we were outside the old city of Avignon and, fleetingly, I longed to be within.

Celia had stopped, putting down her cases (we had not been able to find a porter), and just as I approached her a young man in light trousers and a pale blue shirt came briskly through the dispersing throng. Celia cried 'Paul!' in great surprise. Then she added, in French:

'I expected Oncle Jean or perhaps Gaston. Never . . . I thought you'd be working.'

Paul Gironelle was looking down at her; for a Frenchman he was quite tall, and I – momentarily forgotten – noted at once the look in his eyes and also, with a sense of deep shock, that this was not quite the young man of the photograph. He seemed much thinner and his face looked almost worn; certainly it was a face no longer immature and carefree.

'I've taken a few days' holiday. You might have known that I'd meet you, Célie. The car's over there.'

I thought they had wholly forgotten me, but suddenly Celia turned, beckoning to me.

'Damaris, come here! This is Paul and – this is Damaris Cleveland, my London cousin.' She still spoke in French, apparently without being aware of it, and Paul said in the same language as he took my hand:

'Enchanted, Mademoiselle! We are so pleased that you could come. Célie has often spoken of you.'

We went over to the car, which was a big, expensive-looking one, and Celia said:

'We're honoured! You've borrowed the family car. But you know I like yours, even if she *is* old.'

Paul stopped stowing away the luggage and gave her a very strange look.

'I've sold Marie-Anne,' he said abruptly. 'I've got a motor scooter now.'

'Sold Marie-Anne!' Celia repeated in tones of

horror, then her lips tightened and she climbed into the front seat without another word.

I was already in the back, with some of our luggage beside me, and just as we were driving away she turned to me.

'I'm sorry, Damaris, I've only just realized we've been talking French. But you do speak it quite well, don't you?'

'Oh, I don't mind,' I said hastily in English. 'I shall have to get used to it. I *want* to, only I'm rusty. I'll get better in a few days.' In Paris I had let her do most of the talking.

I hoped they would soon forget me, for I needed time to adjust myself, to get used to the blinding light, the foreign scene, and the presence of Paul.

We were speeding along the road to Tarascon and Arles before Paul spoke again. Then he said, very low, but I heard it:

'It's good to see you again, Célie.'

'I'm glad to be back,' Celia answered and I could see her looking at him covertly from behind her big sun-glasses. I thought that perhaps she too had been shocked by the changed face of her cousin, the laughing young man of the photograph. She had certainly been very much startled and dismayed to hear that he had sold an apparently beloved car. The implication seemed to be that he had needed money very desperately.

Looking back, I think that perhaps it was then, as early as that, that I was aware of the importance of having met Paul Gironelle, but at the time I was only conscious of a vague sadness, a vague excitement, looking at his strong brown neck and the equally brown, long hand that I could just glimpse on the wheel.

I was tired, bewildered, and I didn't really *believe* that I was sitting in a big French car, speeding along the dusty sun-baked road to Arles. We skirted Tarascon and then, long before I expected it, we were approaching Arles. And Celia, who had been very silent, cried:

'Oh, it *is* good to be back! I can't wait to see the Place du Forum and the Alyscamps and, of course, La Vieille Maison.'

'But you didn't intend to come,' he said, still very low.

'No. Well – I had things that needed doing at home. But I'm here now.'

And so intent was I to catch the nuances in that low conversation that we were suddenly in the heart of Arles. I was left with just a vague memory of a section of pale gold city wall and a glimpse of the Place Voltaire. We were driving slowly through streets that had grown very narrow . . . streets where the houses were all of stone, where the sunlight was almost unbearably brilliant and the shadows black, where old women idled on doorsteps and children played dangerously in the dusty gutters. The Rue des Arènes and then one or two streets that were narrower than ever, so that we had to stop altogether to let another car pass.

Ancient, sun-baked Arles on that summer afternoon. . . . I didn't know it then; everything was to come. I still had shreds of my old life about me, yet I was so soon to plunge into another existence.

The car crawled on into what seemed to be a cul-de-sac and I was suddenly much puzzled. La Vieille Maison had gardens and courtyards . . . it was a big house. There was nothing here, in the crowded heart of the town, that could remotely be the house I had pictured. But we were stopping, with the bonnet of the car within a few feet of the high wall that ended the street. On one side, almost tucked into the corner, was what seemed to be the door of a church. On the other side was another door . . . my heart leaped with dismay and astonishment when I saw the words on a plate: 'La Vieille Maison'.

CHAPTER THREE

Damaris in Arles

CELIA CLIMBED out of the car, but I was still fumbling with the door handle. One of the cases had slipped and was holding down my skirt. Paul said, 'Wait, Damaris! I'll open it!' and began to slide out of the driver's seat. At the same moment the door of the church opened and a man came out. I was staring straight past Paul towards him or perhaps I wouldn't have noticed anything. But it was impossible to miss the fact that Paul had tensed all over. I actually saw his neck muscles lock and his face whiten under the tan.

The man – middle-aged, plump, with a little beard – looked, on the contrary, amused. He said: 'Ah, good day, M. Gironelle!' and his dark eyes, catching the sunlight that fell obliquely across the street, leaving our side of it in deep shadow, seemed to flash, or perhaps I only think so now that I know the whole story.

Paul made no acknowledgement at all. He got out of the car, turning towards me, and the man walked away. Paul's face was stiff and inscrutable and there were actually faint lines from nose to chin.

The door was open. . . . I released my skirt and got out and found Celia waiting for me in the shadows of the entrance to La Vieille Maison. Before she could speak the door was flung open and there was a chorus of voices. First came a very handsome middle-aged woman in a pale grey dress, who kissed Celia on both cheeks and held her for a moment in a hard embrace. Behind her was an elderly woman in a white apron whom I knew must be Henriette, who had been with the family since the boys were young children. Behind Henriette, trying to get past us all with murmured greetings and apologies, was the handyman and gardener, Gaston.

'Oh, Tante Lucille! How wonderful to see you again! Henriette, how are you? Gaston, how is your bad leg?'

Gaston shook hands warmly, said that his leg might be worse, and went to help Paul with the luggage, and I found myself being introduced to Mme Gironelle and to Henriette.

We all went into a very dark hall, I still so utterly bewildered by my unexpected surroundings that I had scarcely spoken a word. *This* La Vieille Maison! This dark house in a narrow back street! Dimly I could see flowers on a low polished table . . . shining wooden floors with rugs scattered about. The panelling looked old, the staircase in a corner looked old, too, but—

'This way. You speak French, my dear? It's dark after the sun . . . lighter through here.'

And then we were in a second hall, almost a pleasant living room, with huge windows and a glass door opening on to a flagged terrace. I gasped, for beyond the terrace was a beautiful courtyard, hung with vines and shaded by great trees. There were tables with coloured umbrellas over them . . . pink and purple petunias in stone urns . . . sunlight and shadow making it look like something out of the most exotic film.

'You like it? You think it attractive?' Mme Gironelle had evidently heard my gasp and seen my face. 'Strangers are always surprised, but then Célie must have told you. Welcome to La Vieille Maison, my dear. We are very pleased to have you with us.'

'It's beautiful!' I said, still staring out into the courtyard.

'Ah, but wait! You haven't seen it all. Célie, you have your usual room, of course, and Dam-ar-is –' she seemed to have a little difficulty with the name – 'we've put near you. Henriette—'

The little old woman with the wrinkled, kindly peasant's face smiled at me.

'But of course. This way, Mademoiselle.'

I followed Henriette and Celia out into the court-yard, enchanted with the sweet, hot smells. The nearest trees were familiar friends; I at once recognized their scaly grey trunks. They were plane trees and later I saw them in many other places.

Henriette walked briskly and I was sorry, because I needed to go slowly to take it all in. We walked through a second little court, very shady, as the old stone walls were high, then under a low, rounded archway and into a third, perhaps the most fascinating, the light faintly green from the chestnut leaves overhead.

A lizard darted away into a corner and a ginger cat, flat on its back with four white paws waving languidly in the air, looked up at me with golden-brown eyes. There was complete silence everywhere, except for the twittering of birds, so that it was impossible to believe we were in the heart of Arles. Above, on three sides of the little courtyard, were windows with bright green shutters and I could see the uneven, satisfying angles of orange-red roofs against the dark blue sky.

It was going to be a photographer's paradise and I was deeply glad that I had brought my camera. I am not exactly a keen photographer, but – when I can afford it – I like to take colour pictures. I could quite see that a good deal of money was going to be spent on capturing this scene and many others.

We came to a big whitewashed porch that somehow looked Spanish – perhaps it was the wrought-iron lantern hanging from the low roof and the red flowers in stone pots – and then into a small, highly polished hall with a broad, shallow staircase in one corner. Up the stairs went Henriette and Celia, and I followed, wondering how long it would take me to find my way round this big, spreading house.

Celia flung open a door in the short upper corridor and said:

'It really is good to be back, Henriette. Where are you putting Damaris?'

'She is here.' Henriette led the way round a corner, down two steps and paused before a closed door. Just beside it a steep flight of stairs, almost a ladder, went down into a patch of brilliant sunlight. 'We thought the young lady would like it. And see, Mademoiselle, these steps lead to the garden. You can always go that way if you wish. The door is kept unlocked during the daytime. But have care; the way is steep.'

We all went into my room, which was dark at first because the shutters were closed, but Henriette flung them wide and I looked out into chestnut trees and over low tawny roofs. Below was the third little courtyard and I could just glimpse the middle one through the archway.

'It's absolutely perfect!' I said in English, leaning far out.

'It's really a nicer room than mine,' said Celia. 'But I've had mine so long that I don't want to change. They've actually often tried to make me go into the main building, but I adore it here.'

Henriette beamed at us, said, 'Tea in five minutes, if that pleases you?' and went away, passing Gaston who was bringing my cases.

When he had gone the silence seemed to roll over us and the sweet fragrances came in through the open window. Celia flopped down on the bed, and, coming out of my daze a little, I saw that she looked tired.

'I don't wonder that you love it,' I said. 'I can't believe it's real.'

'This is the oldest part,' she answered, rather absently. 'Part of the old priory. There must have been several priories in Arles. There's even a Rue du Prieuré up near the river. Damaris, I haven't got over the shock yet. I expected a change in Paul, but not to this extent. He's so thin, and to sell his car!' She sighed and rose slowly. 'Better wash and powder our noses.'

'Celia,' I said, as she was going towards the door, 'did you see that man leaving the church as we were getting out of the car?'

She stopped and turned to me, surprised.

'Yes, I did just notice him. Why?'

'I just wondered who he was,' I said lamely. There wasn't time to explain more fully, and she was worried enough.

'I can tell you that. He's a local artist, Jules Maureille. I know him well by sight. He and his brother keep a kind of gallery near the Place du Forum. Of course artists flock to Arles, some good and some bad, but actually his paintings are quite fascinating. Van Goghish. He must do pretty well with them, for at Easter he had a wonderful new car. An American one.'

'Does Paul know him?'

'Oh, well, yes. Just as an acquaintance. I don't think Jules Maureille is very popular in Arles; that's just an impression I have. I must say I was a bit surprised to see him coming out of church. I'd hardly have thought him religious. But maybe he'd been sketching something. He seemed to have a block under his arm. But why the interest?'

She didn't, however, wait for an answer and I was glad. It seemed imperative to put on a thin dress, for I was terribly hot. There was no air at all in the room and when I leaned out of my window briefly again it was even hotter out of doors. The late afternoon sun just caught my window sill with a band of fire.

I opened my cases, pulled out a sun-dress from

under a few thin blouses and washed hastily at the fitted basin. By the time Celia called me from the corridor I was ready. I longed for tea – had Celia perhaps started the Gironelles on this English habit? – but I also urgently needed time to assure myself of my own reality. Paul . . . my reaction to Paul . . . the enchanting house . . . the intense heat . . . the mystery. . . . Oh, soon I must get a chance to think.

But I had to face the Gironelles. When we wandered into the biggest courtyard Mme Gironelle was sitting at a table in the shade with a silver tea service in front of her, and, as we approached, Paul came from the house, with, almost on his heels, a distinguished-looking, grey-haired man. More introductions followed and I found myself liking M. Gironelle very much. I was also relieved to realize that he spoke excellent English; they all did, I found later, but once they were sure that I could manage pretty well in French, that was the language they mainly used.

The tea was weak, with lemon, but very hot, and with it we ate delicious strawberry tarts. I didn't attempt to talk much; I was sufficiently absorbed in watching and listening. It seemed to me that Celia had changed subtly now that she was with her 'second family'; she seemed suddenly un-English, using her hands expressively and talking very rapidly. She had put on a white dress with a low-cut back and her sunglasses somehow added glamour. I knew that Paul was watching her, but Celia was talking to her uncle and aunt and seemed unaware of it.

She was nervous, though; keyed up. Several times she glanced towards the glass door and I realized suddenly that she was waiting for Valérien. It was after five-thirty and I wondered when the shops closed in Arles. While I was wondering this, Valérien appeared, walking swiftly towards us. He was very like his photograph, yet really better looking, perhaps because he was now smiling.

'Célie! So you're here. How are you? Now the family is complete.'

He took her hand, looking down at her, still smiling, and Celia looked up through the dark glasses.

'So I'm part of the family?'

'But of course. You know that you are. Tea! How civilized and welcome. It's hot, even for this time of year.'

He settled himself in the shade and accepted a cup, and conversation flowed fairly easily about our journey and about Celia's summer term in London. She laughed and chattered, but she was still tense. Paul was tense, too. He had stopped looking at Celia and seemed to find it hard to sit still. After a time he excused himself and went away.

Silence followed his going and I saw Celia and her aunt exchange glances. Celia very slightly shook her head. I took advantage of the quiet to ask:

'Would you mind if I explored? I'd like to see the garden.'

'I'm going to unpack,' said Celia, rising also. 'Yes, the garden's lovely, and if you want to slip out into the town without coming back through the house there's an exit beyond the tennis court. Don't get lost!'

Mme Gironelle immediately looked anxious.

'Perhaps you should have company, the first time you go out. Valérien is tired, I think, but Paul—'

'No, I'll be quite all right,' I said firmly. 'I like exploring alone. There's a street map in my guide book and I have a good Michelin map of the district. In a few days maybe I can go somewhere by bus—'

'Or you could use the old bicycle for the nearer places,' said Celia. 'Couldn't she, Tante Lucille?'

'But of course. It's still there in quite good order, I believe. But the traffic in the town—'

'I'll push it out of the town,' I promised. 'But this time I shan't go far.'

'Dinner at eight o'clock,' said Mme Gironelle, still looking as though she was failing a guest.

Celia and I walked away across the courtyard and Celia stopped when we came to the entrance to the second court, pushing open a door in the high wall near us. The blaze of colour beyond dazzled me, for I was not wearing my sun-glasses.

'There you are, Damaris. See you later.' And she went briskly away, her high heels making a clacking sound on the old flagstones.

The garden was a dream. I had never seen a lovelier one in my life. It was just ablaze with zinnias, petunias, salvias and heaven knows what else. The air smelt of lavender and box and there were flowering trees to which I could not give names. The heat and the sun. . . . Oh, grey, wet London seemed a world away.

I wandered along the dusty paths for some time, then found myself beside a wide opening in a high golden wall. The wooden gates were folded back and, beyond a broad shadowy passage, I could see a narrow street. In the passage was the big car that had brought us from Avignon.

With a feeling of high adventure I went out into the street. This was my first real contact with Arles and I savoured it to the full, watching the people, listening to their voices. This was France, there was no doubt about it; everything was a delight, even the smells that, in the ancient heart of the town, were not all pleasant ones.

I didn't want to get lost, so I did take careful note of the street names, and presently I found myself near the great Roman arena, or amphitheatre. The great stone arches loomed above me, with the sky showing through. It looked vast, unbelievably impressive, but I did not want to go inside then. I couldn't cope with it that evening, for I knew it would make an impact.

But the remains of the Roman theatre were different. Presently I could see them through railings – tiers of pale stone and two delicate columns soaring up into the air. I found the gate, paid the entrance fee and wandered under the trees and over the short brown grass until I stood beneath those lovely columns. Perhaps because it was growing late there were only one or two people about. I sat on a hot stone and looked around me, going back nearly two thousand years to when the theatre was in use; when the people of Arles thronged the semi-circles of stone seats to watch a performance.

Sitting there, the past was strangely, heavily upon me, and it was so all the time I was in Arles. The vague menace of ancient history seemed to rise up from the stones everywhere I went, but later I got it mixed up with a menace that was much more modern.

Time was passing, however, and I remembered that I had to unpack and that, in any case, I mustn't be rude and stay away too long from La Vieille Maison. But first I wanted to see the Place du Forum and I found it without difficulty, an attractive square in the heart of the town, with a statue of the poet Mistral in the centre. Everything was just growing lively as the sun went down and people began to come out for drinks and conversation. The café tables were crowded and the scene was quite picturesque.

After that I walked briskly back through streets that had grown shadowy, though no less hot, and, more by luck than good judgement, found the arch-way and was back in the garden of La Vieille Maison. I saw no one as I went through the garden and, between two fig trees, I found the door and the ladder-like stair that would take me straight up to my room. When I got there I realized that I hadn't sorted out my thoughts at all, but I was too hot and bemused to try. I was standing dreamily in the middle of the room when I heard voices in the courtyard below. I didn't take much notice at first, then I realized that it was Celia with – Paul, I thought. Yes, it *was* Paul. She was speaking in quite a low voice, but sound carried on the still air.

'Paul, I can't get used to you like this? What's happened? Why do you look as you do? Oh, I meant to be tactful, but after all I have known you for years.'

'Don't presume on it, Célie,' said Paul, in a voice that was anything but a lover's. 'Mother asked you to come. Oh, naturally I've guessed that. She thought you'd have influence. She guesses how I feel about you. But this is something that concerns only me.'

Celia said a little shakily:

'I don't blame you if you hate me now, but I can't help the way I feel, Paul. I can't *make* myself love you. But I'm very fond of you—'

'Fond!' His voice was very bitter.

'Yes, I am. Of course I am. We grew up together, and if you're in trouble you might let me help.'

'You can't help; no one can. And this is not the place to speak of it, in any case. The little cousin has the room above, I believe—'

'She's gone out.'

I ducked back, guiltily. Of course I shouldn't be listening. I ought to drop something . . . make a noise or else go out of the room. But while I was still hesitating Paul went on:

'Say no more about it. There's nothing you can do, is that clear? I'm in this mess through my own folly and negligence and I deserve it. Try and forget it, please.'

'But, Paul—'

'I'm on holiday until Wednesday of next week. Perhaps we'll go out somewhere if I can borrow the car. You won't refuse to go out with me?'

'Of *course* not, Paul, if you want me to. Oh, I knew

I oughtn't to come; it wasn't fair to you. But I thought if I could help—'

'Save your charity!' said the young man, suddenly almost lightly, and I heard him walking away under the arch. Oh, heavens! Would Celia now come upstairs and find me in my room? But when I looked cautiously out she had paused to light a cigarette and then walked slowly away after Paul. Her shoulders were drooping and she looked desperately unhappy.

When she had gone I leaned on the sill, shaken by the torrent of mixed emotions surging through me. I was sorry for Celia, who not only had to deal with Paul, but endure her secret feelings for Valérien also. Well, presumably they were secret. If Paul guessed that he had a rival, and that rival his brother, he had not hinted as much. Yes, I was sorry for her and puzzled, as she was, by Paul's mysterious trouble, but there was a good deal more. Paul! Already, in a few hours, that rather deep voice meant something to me. vaguely, I disliked Celia for rejecting him, and the vaguely, I disliked Celia for rejecting him and the young man for loving her. I wanted to say to him, 'Don't waste all that good emotion on someone who will never love you in return.' But why should I want to? Why should I care?

Impatiently I washed my hands and put on fresh make-up. By the time I had finished, the early southern dusk had fallen and electric lanterns were making pools of radiance in the courtyards below.

CHAPTER FOUR

The End of Peace

WE HAD dinner out of doors, under a sky thick with stars. The scene was romantic in the extreme and I should have been deeply happy, eating wonderful food, drinking wine, in the hot, velvet night. But I was too much aware of tensions to be wholly happy. Also, of course, I was conscious of being the English stranger and of my occasionally stumbling French. I was shy, naturally enough, though all the Gironelles did their best to put me at my ease.

Even Paul was charming to me. He seemed to have recovered, with whatever effort, a lightness of manner, but the glow from the lamp over the table showed up the faint lines on his face. Valérien was very nice to me too, talking about English books and the plays and films that were on in London just then. He seemed very well aware of what was going on in the wider world.

I began to see that, for some people, Valérien might have a deeper attraction than Paul. But it was the younger brother who held all the attention I had to spare. What *could* be worrying him so much? Could it really be blackmail, and, if so, what had he done? No one could be blackmailed who had not done something very reprehensible. His own folly

and negligence, he had said; that didn't sound like a
very serious crime. Involuntarily I found myself
remembering the man with the beard who had come
out of the church just at the moment when we
arrived. Paul's reaction had been instantaneous;
the artist had looked amused in a not too pleasant
way.

But it would be too much of a coincidence that I
should have seen the cause of the trouble at the very
moment of arrival. *If,* by any chance, Jules Maureille
had something to do with the mystery. He could, of
course, have *planned* to appear then, but how would
he have known that Paul was going to drive up to the
door of La Vieille Maison? No, that was impossible
and I must be over-using my imagination. I jumped
when I realized that Mme Gironelle was asking me
something.

'A little more wine, Damaris?'

'No. No, thank you.' I didn't usually drink wine;
tomorrow I must get up the courage to ask for a fruit
drink instead. I was tired and suddenly very sleepy.
The mosquitoes were dancing overhead, in the light
of the lamp. I stifled a yawn, feeling ashamed.

But they seemed to think it natural that I should
be tired.

'The heat . . . you are unused to it,' said M.
Gironelle. 'And then the long journey, with the train
so crowded. You must go early to bed. But remember,
keep your shutters closed until you turn your light
out or you'll be besieged with mosquitoes all night.
They can't get through the netting in the shutters.'

We had our coffee and then, still a little ashamed,

I excused myself and walked away. The other courtyards were dim and silent . . . the golden cat came
to rub against my legs. I picked him up and stood
there, gazing about me. Last night in Paris; tonight
here, with the Gironelles become reality.

I was in bed in the dark, with the shutters wide
open to show the sky, when Celia came to see me. She
shut the door hastily to keep out the light from the
passage.

'Not asleep yet, Damaris? Have you everything you
want?'

'Oh, yes. I've more or less unpacked. I'm fine.'

'I'm going to bed, too. I'm very tired. Do you like
it here? Does it come up to expectations?'

'I love it,' I said. 'The house is heavenly—what I've
seen of it. I could spend hours just dreaming in the
courtyards and garden.'

'I know. I often do, but you mustn't. You must go
out – see things. I'll come with you sometimes, and
maybe Paul will, too. I can't get anything out of Paul;
I tried, but I'm no wiser. Only it must be something
desperately serious. I had a talk with Tante Lucille.
They've all tackled him, but just had their heads
bitten off. I don't think I'm going to do any good. I
half wish I hadn't come.' And she sighed.

'I – I like your Valérien.'

'He isn't my Valérien, alas,' she said, with another
sigh. 'My only comfort is that no one seems to have
guessed how I feel. He's everything he ought to be;
just himself. But nothing will ever make him wake
up to me. He likes me, he's fond of me . . . glad to
see me. Oh, I'm going to bed!' And she went away,

leaving me staring wakefully at the stars and the dim shapes of leaves, listening to the whine of one mosquito that had managed to find its way in. It was a long time before I even dozed.

I didn't sleep well until dawn, because it was so very hot. Air-conditioning would have been an excellent thing, but I didn't think it was much used in France. Just as the stars were paling and the first faint light was showing through the trees I rose and padded across to lean on the sill. The lamps were out in the courtyards below and they looked dim and dreamlike, like something out of a medieval picture.

I was still leaning there, enjoying a very faint breeze that barely stirred the leaves of the big chestnut nearest me, when I realized that there was a figure under the archway. Whoever it was was standing motionless, only dimly discernible because of something light that it was wearing. It could have been a monk in a white robe and, briefly, my scalp prickled. Then a very modern match flared and I caught a glimpse of Paul's face.

So he couldn't sleep either? It gave me a strange feeling to be sharing the dawnlight with Paul Gironelle. But, even as I watched, he walked softly away towards the middle court and I thought that he must be wearing a light bathrobe.

I went back to bed, feeling cooler, but with my mind once again much disturbed. What *was* it that drove that once gay young man to walk out of doors when he ought to have been asleep?

Surprisingly, perhaps, I did fall asleep soon afterwards and the sun was high when Celia came to wake me.

When we approached the breakfast table in the courtyard Paul was sitting there alone, glancing through a newspaper. He looked rather haggard in the brilliant light and I wondered if he had slept at all, but he smiled at us quite cheerfully and said:

'We've all finished, I'm afraid, but you know, Célie, that breakfast is a movable feast. I'll tell Henriette that you're ready.' And he put the paper over an empty chair and walked away, lithe in his well-cut thin trousers and nylon shirt.

Celia raised her eyebrows at me and lit a cigarette as we waited. It was heavenly in the courtyard on that summer morning. The flagstones had obviously been hosed – and the trees as well – but they were drying rapidly. The sky was again a cloudless dark blue over the tawny roofs. It was like that almost all the time I was in Arles.

I reached for the paper and saw that it was *Le Provençal*. I began to glance idly over the pages, reading items of local news. A famous French playwright had been staying at the Hôtel Romain in Arles . . . there were forest fires in an area not far from Nice . . . someone had been murdered in Marseilles. Then I stiffened with sudden interest, for I had seen a headline: 'Local Artist Spends Busy Summer'. Underneath it I had caught the name Jules Maureille.

M. Jules Maureille, the artist, seems to be even

busier than usual this summer. Apart from helping his brother to run the Galerie Maureille in Arles he has produced a number of paintings. He has already worked at Aix-en-Provence (following in Cézanne's footsteps with several pictures of the Montagne Sainte-Victoire), and at Les Saintes-Maries-de-la-Mer. He is just completing a series of pictures of the Camargue, including one of the abandoned *mas* called Mas Blandois. He tells us that this week end will see the picture of the *mas* completed and then he intends to work for some time in the Roman arena at Arles, making designs for a frieze that is to decorate the walls of a new restaurant in the Place du Forum, to be opened by a cousin of his.

'Something interesting?' Celia asked idly, just as one of Henriette's young helpers in the kitchen appeared with a tray. Celia spoke to Louise in a friendly way, so there was no need for me to answer the question. There was no particular reason for it, but I didn't want to mention my feeling about Jules Maureille. Probably it was all imagination anyway, and she would laugh.

We ate fresh rolls and drank strong, wonderful coffee, and afterwards Celia, who had apparently promised Henriette that she would do some household shopping, wandered off to get the list. I walked in the garden, where Gaston was spraying the flower-bed—*and* the trees, which seemed odd to me—with a long hose, and Paul joined me. This pleased me but made me shy and rather nervous.

'Is this your first visit to France?' he asked.

'No. I've been to Paris,' I said, wishing I knew some way to hold his interest.

'Sometimes I think I'll go and work in Paris,' he said. 'Or leave France altogether. I've an uncle who is a lawyer in West Africa.'

'But – wouldn't you miss Provence?' This idea that he might be planning to go far away was not at all a welcome one.

He shrugged.

'One should see the world, I suppose. One grows restless and I—'

And then Celia joined us, carrying two baskets. She handed the red-and-white one to me.

'We're going marketing. Are you coming, Paul?'

'I'm going to clean the car,' her cousin said rather brusquely, and turned on his heel. We walked out through the archway into the street.

'I *shouldn't* have come,' Celia said. 'Yet one side of me is so glad to be here. I just slip back into it, as though into another self.'

I thought she was right about that other self. It seemed to me that she was indistinguishable from a Frenchwoman as we went from shop to shop and occasionally paused at a market stall, buying bread, vegetables, sewing silk for Mme Gironelle and various other things. She spoke rapid, idiomatic French, took a keen interest in prices and seemed to be known by most of the shopkeepers.

Presently, when most of the marketing was done, she said in quite a different voice and in English:

'We're near Valérien's bookshop. Shall we call in and see him?'

'Of course, if you like,' I agreed. We had already passed a number of excellent bookshops and many shops that sold original paintings and reproductions; Arles seemed a highly civilized and even intellectual place.

Valérien's shop was in the Rue de la République; a double-fronted shop, with an array of English books in one window and a glorious display of travel books in the other. Some of the ones of Provence – very large and probably enormously expensive – filled me with longing. There was one about the Camargue, with a cover picture of white horses galloping along a narrow road between reeds and a distant pattern of umbrella pines against the sky.

Valérien was talking to a customer and we looked around for a while. There were stands of heavenly postcards, both views and art reproductions, and I began to choose colour photographs of Arles to send to my family and friends. Then the customer went and Valérien turned to us, smiling.

'Hullo! You've been shopping, I see. Henriette always says that you get better value than she does, Célie.'

'Henriette flatters me,' said Celia. 'But I always find shopping fun.'

'And Damaris— You are liking Arles?'

'Oh, yes,' I said. 'I'm fascinated.'

After that I went back to choosing postcards, trying to look absorbed. But Celia didn't get much chance to talk to Valérien, because there were a number of customers. Finally a publisher's representative came in and Celia said we'd better go. I paid for the postcards, though Valérien seemed reluctant to take the money.

'Let's go and have a drink in the Place du Forum,' Celia suggested, as we left the shop and walked on the shady side of the street. The pavement was so narrow that we had to walk one behind the other. But when we could talk again she said: 'Val does very well with that shop, especially in summer. He specializes in English books and there are such a lot of American and English visitors nowadays. But his real work is writing. He told me yesterday evening that he's writing a novel now.'

'Celia, he does like you,' I said, for he seemed to me to treat her very warmly, not really casually at all.

'Oh, of course he does,' she agreed impatiently. 'But liking isn't loving. I wish I'd never told you. It makes me self-conscious.'

'It needn't,' I said. 'I do sympathize. He's very nice.' Then suddenly I stopped abruptly, for I had seen the words 'Galerie Maureille'. The gallery was in a very narrow street, with a restaurant on one side and a *patisserie* on the other, but it had quite an air. The lettering over the door was beautifully done and in the window just two pictures were displayed on easels. They were vivid country scenes, with a good deal of flaring ochre and brilliant blue. Van Goghish, certainly. I could see that they were both signed 'Jules Maureille'.

We stopped and looked through the back of the window into the gallery, which was unexpectedly large, with a good display of paintings, not all, I thought, by Jules Maureille. A man was in there walking about, making notes on a pad. I thought at first it was the same man who had come out of the church, but then I realized that he was younger, slimmer, so presumably he must be the brother.

'When I'm rich I shall buy a Maureille,' said Celia. 'They appeal strongly to part of me. The other part prefers someone like Buffet: muted scenes, mud colours. Let's go and buy that drink. I'm dying of thirst!'

So we sat at a table in the Place du Forum and ordered iced fruit drinks. The busy Saturday morning scene gave us plenty to look at and Celia gradually cheered up. She was laughing and talking gaily as we went back to La Vieille Maison.

We lazed for a time after lunch and then Celia said:

'Well, come on, Damaris. You ought to be doing a little sight-seeing.'

'I can go by myself, honestly,' I said, but she laughed.

'In a day or two, maybe. I'm sure you're terribly energetic, even in the heat. But I must see your first reactions to the arena and the Alyscamps.'

So we walked out into the mid-afternoon streets. I was wearing low-heeled sandals and was quite ready to stride out, but Celia wore her usual shoes with very high, thin heels. I carried my camera, which I had already been using in the courtyards and garden of La Vieille Maison.

The great circular walls of the arena soon loomed over us and we walked round to the entrance, where Celia paid for both of us. We entered by way of a dim stone passage, and then there were some steps going upwards. Everything smelt pretty awful and Celia sniffed and laughed.

'Old stones and too many people! There was a bullfight here only a few nights ago. All those thousands of people in the heat.'

'You'd go to one, wouldn't you?' I asked and she looked at me with faint amusement.

'I would, yes. I have been a number of times. That's where my split personality comes in. The English me hates it; the French me is thrilled by the colour and pageantry and doesn't shrink all that much from the blood.'

We came up into the great sunlit blaze of the arena and I was suddenly utterly speechless. I had never imagined anything like it. The tiers and tiers of seats formed a circle round the floor of the arena, and above the topmost seats was a row of open stone arches. The light was dazzling . . . the centre of the floor was ominously stained a rusty colour.

We had entered pretty high and Celia began to go perhaps too quickly down the steps. Suddenly her ankle seemed to give, she hovered for a moment and then fell. Immediately I forgot all about that astonishing scene and rushed to her side. She had not fallen far, luckily, but it had been a heavy tumble.

'Those silly shoes!' I scolded. 'Are you hurt? Oh, Celia!'

Celia raised a very white face.

'I don't know. The steps *are* rather uneven. . . . I *was* silly not to wear comfortable sandals. Wait a minute. . . . I'll sit for a bit.'

The place was scattered with people and an American lady near us came to ask if she could help. Celia waved us both away and settled herself on a seat.

'—all right in a minute, honestly. Just twisted, I expect, and I banged my elbow. It might have been much worse.'

After a few minutes she insisted that she could walk back to La Vieille Maison, though I wanted to go and find Gaston or someone. They could bring the car. . . .

She wouldn't hear of this, however, and eventually she walked very slowly out of the arena and along the Rue des Arènes. For the last few hundred yards she clung to my arm and I was very worried by her obstinacy, sure that she should not be walking on the foot at all.

Henriette and Mme Gironelle received us and there was immediately a good deal of fuss. The doctor was telephoned and Celia was settled on many cushions in the courtyard.

The result of that abortive little excursion was that Celia was soon whisked off to hospital for an X-ray, because the doctor thought she might have fractured a small bone. This turned out to be the case and she was to stay quiet until Monday, when she had to go again and they would probably put the foot and leg in a plaster cast.

Celia was furious and I felt dreadfully guilty. But

she assured me that she knew it was her own fault; that and sheer ill-luck.

'Such a thing to happen! Now I shall be entirely anchored for days, then I suppose they'll let me hobble about on the plaster.'

But maybe it had its compensations, for Valérien sat beside her in the courtyard all evening. They were still there, talking, long after we had finished our coffee and dispersed.

I walked in the garden, looking at the young moon and thinking about Paul, who had seemed more abstracted and tense than ever at dinner.

And that Saturday evening, my second evening in Provence, was really the end of peace.

CHAPTER FIVE

What Happened on the Camargue

BY THE middle of Sunday morning I had admitted to myself that I was strongly attracted to Paul. Really I had fallen in love at first sight, or perhaps even earlier when I looked at his photograph. My whole being was filled with amazement and wonder, warmth and pain; I had never experienced anything like it before. It was a shattering revelation to realize how much pleasure there might be in merely being in someone's presence, watching the movement of his hands, the line of his profile, listening to his voice. And the pain, of course, was because, though Paul was perfectly polite, he simply didn't know I was there – a real person, sharply aware of him. On Sunday morning, the little he was with us, he didn't even take much notice of Celia. He seemed entirely lost in what must certainly have been unpleasant thoughts.

I sat in the garden by a huge flowering lavender bush, in the shade of a feathery tamarisk, and tried to think. And the only conclusion I could come to was that somehow I had to find out about Paul's mystery and try and help. But how to start? I had no clues, unless one could count the vague feeling I had about the artist, Jules Maureille.

Maureille! The paper had said he would be

painting on the Camargue and I wanted to see the Camargue in any case. The news item had mentioned a deserted *mas*; I knew that this meant a kind of ranch house. The Michelin map with the Camargue on it was in my bag and I opened it and spread it out. The name of each *mas* seemed to be marked and after only a short search I found the one that had been mentioned. It was only about seven or eight miles from Arles, just off a little side road.

Well, there could be no harm in cycling in that direction. I could be the English stranger exploring interesting country – true enough – and maybe I could go and photograph the *mas* and, if he was there, perhaps get into conversation with the artist. It was at least worth trying, though I hardly knew what I expected from any such encounter.

After lunch, when Celia was settled in the big courtyard, writing letters, Valérien was also writing, presumably his novel, in the third court, and Paul was heaven knew where, I went in search of Mme Gironelle. By then I knew my way about the big, rambling house pretty well and I had learned that I didn't need to walk through the courtyards to get from my bedroom to the main building. A narrow corridor with some old beams brought me into the broad upper landing and there was Tante Lucille, arranging zinnias in a pewter jug.

When I told her that I was going out cycling she immediately looked rather distressed.

'You are sure you will be safe? Really someone ought to go with you, my dear. Such a young girl . . . but Valérien is so busy with his writing and Paul –

well, he goes his own way these days. It distresses me
very much, you understand. When we have a guest,
and poor Célie is unable to move, one would
think—'

'Oh, please don't worry. I'm used to going about
alone. I like it. I'm going to take photographs and
that's always better alone. Other people get impatient. And I told Celia when she said I could come
here that I wouldn't want entertaining.'

Her handsome, worried face suddenly puckered.

'We are glad to have you. Even to have a new face
about the house has made us a little more cheerful.
Célie says she has told you; perhaps, in any case, you
would have realized that all isn't well. We are having
a troubled time. . . . Paul. But he doesn't consult any
of us. Though so light and easy in manner he was
always, at heart, a reticent boy. He never confided.
One perhaps knows that children rarely confide in
their parents, but it hurts when there is real trouble.
Well, you go along, my dear, but take care. The
bicycle is in the shed by the tennis court, with Paul's
motor scooter.'

'Thank you. And – and I'm so sorry about it all,'
I stammered, finding it difficult to know what to say.

I hurried back to my room to fetch my camera and
sun-glasses, then went straight down into the garden
by way of my steep stairs, so as not to disturb
Valérien. From my window I could see that he was
very much absorbed.

The bicycle was old, but it seemed to have been
recently oiled and the tyres were hard. I was just
wheeling it towards the stone arch when someone

called me and I saw Louise hurrying across the garden with a flask and a small package in her hands.

'Mademoiselle! Henriette says here is an iced drink and some cake.'

I thanked her warmly and put them, with my hand-bag, in the basket on the front of the bicycle. Then I went out into the streets of Arles. The Rue de la République took me towards the Pont de Trinque-taille and presently I saw the River Rhône in front of me, wide there, for it was not so many miles from the sea. It wasn't very picturesque at that point, even rather industrial, but I was soon over the bridge and leaving Trinquetaille behind me.

There was not a great deal of traffic on the road that led into the Camargue and I sped rapidly along, glad that my own speed created a faint, very hot breeze. And gradually, except for an occasional car, I had the whole vast scene to myself and I began to feel the strangeness of that country. The dark blue sky seemed higher, arching enormously over the white saltings, the tall beds of reeds and the rice fields. Occasionally there was a sluggish stream, perhaps arched by an old stone bridge, or a little whitewashed house with a red roof, or sometimes a thatched one, that I thought must be a *cabine de gardian*. I saw no white horses or black bulls, and no flamingoes either, but there were dragonflies in their thousands, enormous ones of many colours.

For a time I even forgot my original purpose in riding that way. It was enough to be free, in summer, in that wonderful, peculiar country. Occasionally, in the distance, I saw a big *mas*, usually sheltered from the mistral by a line of umbrella pines, but I knew that so far I had not sighted the one I was seeking.

Presently I took a side road and now there were no cars at all. The reeds shut out most of the view, but I knew that I must be getting near. And almost before I expected it I saw a kind of drive, with an old white gate folded back, and there was a small broken sign that said 'Mas Blandois'. I could see the ranch house in the distance, a big place, whitewashed like most of the buildings, with a very red roof. It might be deserted, but it didn't look ruined. I propped up my bicycle and stood on one of the rungs of the gate to get a better view, and then my heart leaped, for there was a car parked by the out-buildings, a big pale green car. It was some distance away, but it could easily have been an American car. It seemed pretty certain that Jules Maureille was painting there.

The silence was intense, except for the humming of insects; the reeds were quite motionless on the road behind me. I found myself very unwilling to carry out my original plan immediately. Besides, I was hot and thirsty. So I went on a few yards along the road, dropped my bicycle against a bank, where it at once sank down in the grass and flowers, and, with Henriette's iced drink in my hand, looked round for a shady place to sit. The reeds cast the only faint patches of shade, so I found a small gap and settled myself. It felt like having a forest on three sides, but I could just see the gate that led to Mas Blandois and a few yards of the road beyond.

The ice-cold lemonade was absolutely delicious, but I made myself keep half of it to have with the cake later. I sat there dreamily, with dragonflies flitting past me, trying to get up the courage to go and photograph that big building a few hundred yards away. In that vast solitude I knew that I wasn't keen on coming face to face with the artist, but I told myself that it was absurd to feel uneasy. He could do nothing to me; in fact he probably wouldn't even notice me. It was silly to have too much imagination.

And then the totally unexpected happened, so that I could hardly believe my eyes. For it seemed that I had sudden, irrefutable proof that my imagination – rather than leading me astray – had put me on the right lines. I heard the low sound of a small engine and a motor scooter came round the corner about fifty yards away. Riding it was Paul, and when he came to the gate of Mas Blandois he stopped, hesitated for perhaps five seconds, then got off his machine and began to push it towards the distant building.

I found myself on my feet, with my heart pounding wildly. Paul of course had read the paper that gave news of Jules Maureille. There could be only one possible reason for him to come to Mas Blandois this week end and that was because he wished to speak to the artist. Yet on Friday, when they had come face to face, he had certainly looked as though speech was the last thing he would want with him. Well, perhaps not in public, in front of a stranger. And there was no doubt that he could hardly have discovered greater solitude than in this almost deserted tract of the Camargue.

I put the flask back in my basket, and with my handbag hanging on my arm and my camera over my shoulder, I set off to walk towards the group of buildings by the umbrella pines. If Paul had looked back he would have seen me, but he didn't. He propped the scooter up by one of the out-buildings and, after a moment's hesitation, disappeared round the house.

Curiosity and determination now held me in a strong grip. I had forgotten fear, though I was dimly aware of the brooding darkness of the pines. For *someone* had to know about Paul – *I* had to know. For knowing, I felt with quite unjustified optimism, I might be able to help and so release him from that trance of worry and fear. And if he were released, his old self, he might look at me as a person, might even forget Celia.

But I didn't quite know how to proceed. If I followed Paul I might come face to face with the pair of them and that would be a disaster. I could say that I was taking photographs, and later I could ask Paul what the artist was to him, but he wouldn't tell me and I should be no further forward.

The one-time dwelling loomed over me, white and deadly silent in the dazzling heat of the southern afternoon. The front door was shut, but, on investigation, not locked. It had been once, but someone had forced the lock; maybe a tramp looking for a night's lodgings.

The interior seemed very dark and I took off my sun-glasses, blinking to try to get my eyes used to the gloom. I had stepped straight into a big high room, a room that, even abandoned and dusty, had some pretensions to beauty. The walls were white, the high ceiling was beamed and there was a huge open fireplace. The windows were boarded up, except at the very top, and it was through these gaps that the light came in.

Holding my breath, I walked softly in my rubber-soled sandals until I stood underneath the nearest window. I could hear nothing at first, then suddenly there was the sound of voices, too far away for me to make out any words.

Quickly, on tiptoe, I ran across to a staircase and mounted it to the upper floor. Here the windows were not boarded and I went softly and cautiously into a room at the back. The big window was not only unboarded, it was broken, and, advancing with the utmost care, I could see Jules Maureille standing by an easel and Paul with him. They were both some distance away, but now I could hear. For one thing, Paul's voice had risen to an almost hysterical pitch.

'I've told you already – I have no more money! I sold the car, didn't I? I've raised every penny I possibly can and you aren't satisfied. I suppose blackmailers are always like that, but you must *know* . . . you don't really want my money. I must be the least paying proposition you have. Don't tell me there are no others, for I should not believe you.'

The artist was silent for several moments, merely looking at the taut young man with a kind of amused pleasure, very nasty to watch.

'Nevertheless, my dear M. Gironelle, you will find more money or you know well what will happen. An anonymous letter to the police, and then they will feel it necessary to question you, and you, being basic-ally an honest citizen, will then confess. You see, I understand your psychology. Your career would be over and your name ruined in Arles. And in your profession you certainly can't afford it. You hope to be a successful lawyer, you are ambitious—' He had a quite hateful voice. I knew he was thoroughly enjoy-ing baiting the helpless young man who stood before him, and Paul knew it too. He said in a choked voice:

'It's a war of nerves, so that you can see me squirm. How I wish I'd gone to the police in the first place. Everywhere I go in Arles I seem to see your evil face. On Friday— Why were you coming out of the church just at that moment? It wasn't an accident, though I don't see—'

'I have my spies,' said Jules Maureille with calm pleasure.

'Someone will – will murder you one day, Maureille!'

The artist smiled and then made a careful stroke on the picture before him.

'I hardly think so. To murder takes courage or a degree of folly or madness that few people possess. You are already in enough trouble, *n'est-ce pas?* If I may make a suggestion you could ask your father for money. He's rich, without much doubt, and he wouldn't wish to see one of his sons dragged through the mud.'

'Ask my father. . . . That's the last thing I'd do! I got into this mess myself and somehow I'll get out of it again. But I warn you, Maureille—'

'Shall we say just a token – perhaps a thousand francs by Thursday? Delivered in the usual way.'

Paul made a strange, almost animal sound and then spun round on his heel and strode away. I watched him walk round the building and so out of sight, then, still crouching well back, I watched the artist settle down to work. He was whistling softly and the tune was that innocent and charming song, 'Sur le Pont d'Avignon'. I felt that I would never like it again.

Somehow I got myself downstairs and back to the front door. Paul, riding his scooter, was just disappearing towards the gate.

I almost ran back to the road, quite unaware then of the heat. I flung myself back in my shady corner amongst the reeds and tried to think. But my thoughts got me nowhere. *I* couldn't lend Paul as much as a thousand francs, and, even if I could, it would only lead, obviously, to further demands. It was quite clear to me that Jules Maureille was enjoying his victim's suffering and it seemed unlikely that he would cease to ask for money.

'Paul! Oh, Paul!' I said to myself, feeling more pain and bewilderment than ever before in my life. 'What did you do? Was it something so very terrible? And what is going to happen in the end?'

The dragonflies flittered before my face, the reeds cracked dryly as I pressed back against them. The Camargue had lost some of its magic. I felt menace everywhere.

CHAPTER SIX

The Meeting with Thomas

I DON'T KNOW how long I sat there. It must have been quite a long time. But at last I realized that, in spite of everything, I was hungry and thirsty. I finished the iced drink and ate the cake and then – impelled by I scarcely knew what motive – I walked back a little way towards Mas Blandois and took two photographs. After that, restless, not quite knowing what I wanted to do, I left the bicycle where it was and walked on along the narrow road.

I took two more pictures: one, where the high reeds ended for a time, of the saltings and rice fields and a distant white *cabine,* and one of some flamingoes by a pool. That was lucky, but I wasn't in the mood to be triumphant. My mind was still filled with all I had learned and with a sort of sick horror whenever I remembered Paul. I wanted him to be safe and happy again. Oh, how passionately I wanted it! Yet I think I knew then that the thing would lead to real tragedy.

At last I turned and walked back to my bike. I had had enough of the Camargue for one day and suddenly I wanted the crowded, animated streets of Arles. I couldn't imagine why I had lingered there, alone under the blazing sky. But I seemed not to have been quite myself; I had been lost in a haze of fear and doubt since I overheard that dreadful, frightening conversation.

I began to ride slowly back towards the main road, bumping a little over the stony, uneven surface. I heard a car behind me, but I heard it only vaguely. Then suddenly there was a loud blast from the horn and I glanced over my shoulder to find it almost upon me: a huge pale green car that took up most of the available space. Just beside me there was a water-filled ditch so I could not pull over much. In any case there was hardly time, for the car was coming so quickly. It went past, brushing within inches of me and just for a moment I was conscious of a familiar face looking at me, smiling.

Then the car was gone in a cloud of dust and I was left wobbling frantically on the edge of the ditch, completely taken aback and demoralized. The front wheel caught a stone and it was impossible to save myself. I fell off at the very edge of the ditch, with the front wheel of the bicycle actually splashing into the water. The water shot up and went into my eyes and I was aware that I had jarred myself badly, and painfully scraped my knee. At the same time I realized vaguely that there was another car . . . it had stopped. I heard a door slam and then footsteps. A pleasant English voice cried:

'Good heavens! Are you hurt? That bounder nearly took your ear off: I saw it all. Er, I mean – *Mademoiselle, avez-vous*—?' And he changed to quite fluent French, repeating most of what he had said.

I struggled into a sitting position and stared up into a young, good-looking face. He had fair curly hair, blue eyes and seemed to be two or three years older than I.

'Oh, don't worry. I'm English, too,' I said. 'I— No, I don't think I'm much hurt. My knee looks a bit of a mess, but it's only scraped. I hope I haven't bust the bike because it isn't mine.'

'An English damsel in distress!' he cried, smiling very nicely. He helped me up, dusted the back of my dress, and then heaved the bicycle upright, testing the tyres and chain. 'No, it seems O.K. Just a bit wet. Look! I took the number of that car. American make, wasn't it? The blighter was going much too fast—'

'He didn't actually touch me. It was really my own fault that I fell. Yes, it was an American car, but it's owned by a local. He did it on purpose, I think, out of – mischief.' I remembered the face that had glanced at me briefly and was as sure as I could be that Jules Maureille had recognized me as the girl who had been in the Gironelles' car. He couldn't know more than that; he couldn't have seen me at Mas Blandois. He had never once glanced up at the window and I thought I had kept well back.

'Mischief seems hardly the word. Mean you know the brute?'

'By sight. He's a local artist. Not a very nice man, I gather. He did look – amused.'

'For two pins I'd report him to the police for dangerous driving.'

'Oh, you'd better not do that. I'm not hurt.'

'No, but you're shaken and you *might* have been. Are you on holiday in Arles?'

'Yes. I'm from London. I'm staying with the Gironelles at La Vieille Maison. I came on Friday.'

He whistled.

'La Vieille Maison? That's a bit of a show place, isn't it? I've heard the name.'

'I'm with my cousin, who is related to the Gironelles.'

'Well, look here. You're hot and you look upset. You don't want to cycle all the way back to Arles. Let me put the bike in the back of the car.'

I hesitated, glancing from him to the rather old open car that was so obviously British. I didn't usually accept lifts from strange men. He seemed to realize why I was hesitating, for he went on quickly:

'Honestly, you'll be all right. I'm Thomas Gray. I'm a Londoner, too. A modern languages student; one more year to go. I've taken a job in Arles to perfect my French. I'm working at the Hôtel Romain at the reception desk. Respectable, hard-working (mostly) and— Oh, come on back to Arles and let's have some tea or something. You do look shaken.'

I liked him at once and I knew I could trust him. He was that kind of person; it stuck out a mile. So I told him my name and agreed to the lift and tea. The bicycle was put in the back of the car, where it wobbled a little, and I climbed in beside him. We drove off and in a very short time were over the bridge and in Arles. But before we got there I had learned a little more about him. He had been bird-watching on the Camargue (it was one of his hobbies), he lived in St John's Wood and – this slight coincidence at once seemed to make our unconventional meeting quite all right –

had been at the same school as Nancy's brother Ronald, but a couple of forms below him.

'I'm back on duty at six,' he said, as he parked the car in the Boulevard des Lices and we found an empty café table. The impressive frontage of the great Hôtel Romain was only just a little way up the boulevard on the other side.

'What a huge place!' I said. 'Do you enjoy working there?'

'Well, it's interesting. A good opportunity of observing types. Of course I have to speak a lot of English, because we get plenty of British and Americans, but I take every opportunity to speak French, German and Italian as well.'

After all my mixed emotions when in the presence of Paul, and the strangeness and terror of the afternoon, he was a very soothing companion. Not dull, though; he began to talk most amusingly about some of the people he had met. Yet I began to long to see Paul again and to be back at La Vieille Maison, so I didn't linger when we had finished our tea. I insisted that I would walk the rest of the way, pushing the bicycle, so Thomas lifted it out of the car. Then he looked at me and asked:

'Couldn't we meet again, Damaris? I'd like it very much. I'm free on Tuesday afternoon at two and we could go somewhere in the car. You ought to get around and as you say your cousin's hurt her foot and the others are busy—'

I was by then dying of impatience to get back, but I really did like Thomas and it seemed quite possible that I would be glad of a sane English friend, someone who was not caught up in the Gironelles' troubles. So I said:

'All right, so long as they don't arrange something for me. I'll come here, to this café.'

'You could come and have coffee or something at the hotel. They have tables under the trees and on the terrace.'

But I didn't feel quite equal to facing that imposing façade, with its huge pillars and uniformed doormen, so we settled on the café and I said good-bye and hurried away. My knee was just a little stiff, but I didn't think it was anything at all to worry about. I certainly wasn't going to confess that I had had a tumble.

On the way back to La Vieille Maison I could think of nothing but what my next course of action should be. I had learned the truth through my own curiosity, or maybe plain inquisitiveness, and certainly I didn't seem to be any better off with my dreadful new knowledge. I was still filled with alarm and even terror, terror for Paul, who had seemed so helpless, so vulnerable, in the presence of Jules Maureille. All it had done so far was to make me see that I was certainly in love with Paul. I had the crazy certainty that I didn't care what he had done; whatever it was I would stick by him.

But, as I walked into the garden of La Vieille Maison, once more cold awareness came over me. Paul hardly knew I existed; he probably wouldn't even *want* me to stick by him. What I had learned I ought to keep to myself.

I slipped straight up to my room, showered (I forgot to say that there was a shower just near my room), and changed. When I went out through the courtyards the evening was already growing shadowy and Valérien was no longer working. I found the whole family in the biggest courtyard having pre-dinner drinks. Valérien was there and Paul, and Celia was sitting as she had been doing when I left, propped up with cushions and with her injured foot encased in a soft nest of them. But she had changed her dress, so someone must have helped her up to her room.

I was met with quite a chorus of greetings.

'We were growing quite worried about you, my dear,' said Mme Gironelle. 'Did you have an enjoyable afternoon? Where did you go?'

'Yes, I enjoyed it very much,' I said. 'I went on to the Camargue and took some photographs. I saw some flamingoes. It's a most fascinating area, isn't it?'

In the midst of that civilized scene, in the charming courtyard, the events of the afternoon began to seem fantastic, dreamlike. I glanced at Paul and saw that he seemed to have recovered his assurance if not his spirits. His face didn't change when I made my remarks. He had no idea that I had been there at Mas Blandois.

Sooner or later I might tell him, but for a time it must be my secret. The only person I might have told was Celia, but she looked white and strained and admitted that her foot had been hurting her.

I did my best to behave normally for the rest of the evening, but it was difficult and I was very, very glad when I could escape to my room, but not to sleep. I leaned on my window sill for a long time, standing there in the dark, wondering where it would all end. For end it somehow must. It was all too clear that Paul could not keep on paying sums of money to Jules Maureille.

I dreamed of the artist, constantly seeing his mocking, subtly evil face. Once I was locked in a room with him in the deserted *mas* . . . once he was chasing me in the car while I desperately tried to make the bicycle go faster. I was glad when morning came, for the sunlight seemed to dispel most of the nightmares and I did manage to sleep dreamlessly for a couple of hours.

M. Gironelle took Celia off to the hospital and I offered to do some shopping for Henriette. I found this quite fun and I was determined to do it well, if not as efficiently as Celia, so for a time my thoughts were occupied. But about eleven o'clock, when I had bought everything on the list, I found my feet taking me towards the Galerie Maureille. It was a kind of compulsion. I didn't want to go, but go I did. I walked slowly towards it and stood looking at the pictures in the window. They had been changed since Saturday morning and now there were two pictures of Arles on display: one of the Place du Forum and one of the ruins of the Roman theatre.

With a little thrill of fear I saw that both the Maureilles were in the gallery, but Jules seemed to be ready to leave. He was carrying an easel, canvases and paints and also a small bag that looked as though it contained his lunch. The door was open and I heard him saying:

'Well, Justin, I'll be off. Charles will be along to help you this afternoon, as you know.'

'You'll be roasted in the arena today. It's hotter than ever.'

'You know I enjoy the heat. And I want this brilliant light.' He was coming out; I tried to move, I meant to, but my legs held me there. I stared fixedly at the picture of the Place du Forum, apparently lost to the world. And so I heard him add, in a low voice: 'She's the girl who is staying at La Vieille Maison. English, I think. Quite a nice-looking piece, wouldn't you say?'

Perhaps he thought I didn't understand French. But would he have minded, in any case? I did turn then and walk very slowly away towards the corner, trying to look as though I hadn't a care in the world, but my face was burning. 'Quite a nice-looking piece' indeed! I hated his voice . . . and everything about him.

Celia came back from the hospital with her foot and most of her leg in plaster and the information that she could start to try and walk on it in twenty-four hours' time. She said to me:

'It *is* sickening, and I feel guilty about you, Damaris. You don't seem very happy. Are you bored?'

'I'm quite all right. No, I'm not bored.'

'I thought something had upset you yesterday. You looked a bit odd to me.'

'You imagined it,' I assured her lightly.

'Well, in a day or two M. Gironelle is going to take the pair of us around in the car. He wants you to see

Nîmes and the theatre at Orange – it's far more complete than the one here. A glorious place.'

'That would be nice, but actually I may go somewhere tomorrow. I've a date in the afternoon.' And then I told her a carefully edited story about my meeting with Thomas and stressed how nice he was. Celia looked rather troubled.

'Well, I suppose it's all right. I feel kind of responsible for you. You ought not to pick up any young man.'

'He isn't "any young man"; he really is nice. I'll bring him to meet you some time soon.'

'Well, where are you going this afternoon? I wish Paul would take you somewhere, but he said something about calling into his office with some work he brought home. I haven't got anywhere at all with Paul. He's a complete clam, shut up in his shell. Oh, if only I wasn't so *helpless*. There must be something to find out, if only one knew where to look.'

I remembered guiltily all I had found out, but by then I had definitely decided to keep it to myself for the time being. So I changed the subject, saying that I might go to see the Alyscamps and maybe St Trophime's church and cloister. But when I set off my unruly feet promptly took me towards the arena. After all, I hadn't seen it properly on the day when Celia had her accident and I wanted to take some photographs. I still had about three exposures on the film that had been in my camera when I left England. I had begun it at school, when I took some pictures on Sports Day.

It was breathlessly hot and I walked quite slowly, stopping on the way to buy a new colour film. I went slower than ever when, as I was approaching the entrance to the arena, I saw Paul in front of me. He was carrying some kind of big briefcase and he certainly looked in no hurry. Once he almost stopped, as though he had changed his mind, then he went on more briskly.

I supposed that his office must be somewhere past the arena and I expected him to go on, past the parked cars and motor coaches. But to my surprise he turned, after further hesitation, towards the entrance. A large party of people was just coming out and another crowd – Americans, they seemed to be – had just arrived by coach. They were surging towards the pay booth, marshalled by a tall man wearing horn-rimmed glasses.

I was almost up to the entrance by then and for a few moments I lost Paul in the crush, then I saw him just disappearing along the dark passage. He had not bothered to pay; perhaps, as a resident, he didn't have to, or else he'd not felt like waiting in a long queue.

I wondered why on earth he was going into the arena, but of course there was only one possible explanation. He knew that Jules Maureille would probably be painting there and maybe he wanted to see him again. Perhaps he had managed to raise the money and wanted to give it to him, but would he do so in such a public place? It had sounded as though they had some set arrangement about paying.

I must have looked impatient, standing there at the back of the crowd, for the man in horn-rims looked back and said to me:

'You'd better go first, I guess. I have to buy thirty-eight tickets—'

'Thirty-seven,' said someone. 'Mrs Schwartz has gone shopping.'

'And Mr Smith said he'd kind of had enough of Roman remains and—'

'Gee! I'd better count you all again. You go right ahead,' to me.

So I paid the entrance fee and hurried the way Celia and I had gone on Saturday. Actually, as I soon realized, there was quite a maze of passages at different levels inside the walls of the arena, with exits giving on to the different blocks of seats. But I went straight up the stairs and came out fairly high, once more amazed and dazzled by the vast glare of the place, by its immensity, its paleness under the sun. However, I was only thinking about this with one part of my mind, for there, in the very centre of the arena, sat Jules Maureille, his canvas before him on an easel. He was painting absorbedly; a conspicuous figure on the empty floor of that great place.

Quite a number of people were scattered about, but they scarcely impinged on the scene. After all, the arena would hold many thousands of spectators during a bullfight. From where I was standing I could see all around, but there was certainly no sign of Paul in his pale yellow shirt. My eyes raked every group, every section of seats, and he was not there. Every time someone emerged from one of the dark openings around the arena my heart leaped, but it was never Paul.

So perhaps he had changed his mind and gone out again. Probably, when he saw the conspicuous position the artist was in, he had given up all thought of speaking to him. At any rate, though I must have been in there five minutes, he had still not put in an appearance.

Jules Maureille continued to paint, apparently totally disregarding the fact that his solitary figure could be a target for all eyes. Perhaps, if he was aware of it, it pleased him. He seemed to me to be that kind of person.

Well, I had come ostensibly to take photographs, so I might as well get on with it. I waited until a whole stretch of the arena was without people and then took one, aiming high to get in the topmost arches. Then I took another sideways across the seats and afterwards began to wander slowly round, though the space between the rows of seats was narrow. I still had not taken one across the floor of the arena, but if I did so I must get Jules Maureille in the picture and I didn't really want any record of that unpleasant man.

Yet he somehow exercised a powerful fascination; I felt a little like a creature facing a snake, though he was not looking at me. He seemed to be painting in some detail, for he was not glancing up at all. I moved a little farther round until I was almost exactly facing him. If he looked up now he was bound to see me, isolated in the middle of an empty block of seats.

I sat down, with the camera ready on my knee. I knew that I would have to take that picture, yet I was putting it off. I almost willed him to look up, though the very thought of him doing so filled me with a strange kind of alarm. He knew me . . . he had deliberately tried to drive me into the ditch. But that, I was sure, had just been his own particular kind of malice. I must really mean almost nothing to him.

Then I was alone no longer. The whole party of Americans streamed out of the dark opening above me and spread, laughing and chattering, over the seats.

'Guess, if you'll all sit down, this will be the moment to tell you something about it,' said the tall guide. But they went on fussing and laughing, making loud comments.

I didn't want to stay there any longer. I stood up abruptly, raised my camera and took the photograph almost without focusing it or being sure what I had in the picture. At precisely that moment a sharp crack rang out. The noise echoed and re-echoed round the circular place, and, totally unbelieving for a moment, I saw that Jules Maureille had slumped forward against his canvas.

For just a few seconds he huddled there, then the easel went over and the body of the artist rolled down on to the floor of the arena, exactly where it was still stained from the last bullfight.

CHAPTER SEVEN

Death in the Arena

I DON'T KNOW how long there was complete silence, except for the sound of the shot still reverberating around the pale stones; then several people screamed. From all parts of the arena people began to surge forwards and downwards.

But I only wanted to get away from the place. I was thinking, in a terrified, confused way, of Paul, whom I had seen entering the building. Anyone who stayed might be questioned and I couldn't afford to be questioned about Jules Maureille. Though I had actually seen nothing; I had been taking the photograph just at the very second when the shot rang out.

Still, it would be safer to leave . . . not to get involved. And there was no difficulty at all about that. No one took the least notice of me as I gained the dark passage and ran round inside the walls, calming my pace a little when I remembered Celia's injured foot. It wouldn't help if I were to damage mine. I could hear shouts and commotion in the distance, but there was no one about when I approached the entrance. Even the ticket booth was empty, so presumably the attendants had gone to see what had happened.

In a few moments they would be telephoning the police, but meanwhile the coast was clear. Outside, however, there was another large party – Germans this time – assembling round their leader. He was discoursing loudly, waving his hand at the high arches. None of them even glanced in my direction and I walked casually away, but I didn't seem to breathe at all until I had put several hundred yards between myself and the arena.

I had reached the public gardens before I realized that I had not turned towards La Vieille Maison. Beyond the gardens the traffic roared along the Boulevard des Lices, and in the boulevard was the Hôtel Romain. I was terribly shaken, my legs felt like jelly, and the memory of Thomas's sanity and friendliness drew me on. He had mentioned coffee at the hotel and I had to have something. I could see why people felt they needed brandy after a shock. But strong coffee would do.

The heat on the exposed side of the Boulevard des Lices was so intense that I felt a little faint and I crossed as soon as I could and walked thankfully in the shade. My footsteps faltered as I approached the entrance to the hotel, but it was the middle of the afternoon and everything seemed to be wrapped in the calm of a siesta. The traffic rumbled and roared, but there were empty tables under the trees and along a terrace, even between the pillars of the front entrance. There was not even a doorman in sight.

I pushed open the swing doors and found myself in a huge hall that seemed cool after the heat out of doors. It was dark, too, and it took me a moment to see the desk and Thomas – quite alone – looking at me over the counter.

'Damaris!' he cried. 'How nice to see you! But—Is something wrong? Don't say you've fallen off your bike again?'

'No, I haven't been on it today. I was – was in the arena taking photographs and someone was shot. That artist who nearly ran me down yesterday. He was painting in the very middle and suddenly there was a shot and he slumped down . . . just where they have the bullfights, Thomas. I – I'm sure he was dead!'

'Good heavens!' He took another look at me. 'What a thing to happen! Who shot him? Did you see?'

I could answer that honestly.

'No, I didn't see anyone. Well, only all the Americans round me, who were just going to be lectured by their leader. I was taking a picture when I heard the shot. Everyone was going towards him, but I – I came away. I couldn't bear it and no one stopped me.'

'Quite the best thing you could have done,' he said reassuringly. 'You only saw what everyone else must have done; probably not as much, as you were using your camera. You don't want to get involved with foreign police. Look here! You'd better have something; you look very white. What would you like?'

'Coffee, please,' I said. 'Strong black coffee. I – I—It did make me feel rather queer.'

He pressed a bell and a waiter came to take the order. Thomas waved to a table not far from the desk.

'Sit there. It's cooler inside. And it's the doldrumy part of the afternoon. It's deadly being on between two and five. But useful that I'm here today.'

'I – I don't know why I came,' I said.

'Very sensible of you. I'm so glad you did.' The telephone rang then and he turned to answer it, so I began to change the film in my camera. It was good to have something to do and it looked as though Thomas would be occupied for quite a few minutes. He was looking up dates and making entries in a large book, with the receiver still held to his ear with one hand.

When he had hung up again he turned back to me.

'So someone bumped that blighter off? Perhaps he'd driven someone else into a ditch, or worse. What do you know about him?'

'N-nothing much. He paints Van Goghish pictures and seems quite successful, and he helps his brother to run the Galerie Maureille, where they sell his and other paintings. It was in the paper – *Le Provençal* – that he'd be painting in the arena, so I suppose anyone could have known.'

'Maureille? Oh, yes, I read that bit, but it didn't mean much to me then. Well, I suppose the police will get whoever did it. After all, the Roman arena is rather a public place to choose for a murder. One has to pass ticket booths going in and coming out.'

My coffee came then. When the waiter had gone and I had taken a comforting drink, I said:

'It seems like it, on the face of it. But there were several big parties, especially when I went in. Anyone could — could have slipped past. And when I left, the attendants had evidently gone to see what had happened.' The very thought of Paul made me feel terrible again and I must have looked queer because Thomas said concernedly:

'It really has upset you. I should go home when you've drunk your coffee and lie down for a while. It's a nasty thing to happen.'

Far nastier than he knew. If we had been in a less public place I might have blurted out the whole awful story, trusted him with it, but various people passed through the hall and then a party of three arrived and had to register, filling in the little forms that foreigners often suffer from in France. By the time a porter had led them away I'd finished my coffee and it seemed better to go.

Thomas came to the door with me and I looked at him gratefully. He was wearing a formal suit and looked quite different from the sun-tanned and casually dressed young man of the previous day, but he was just as nice as I had thought at first.

'Thank you for listening. I feel better now.'

He took my hand briefly, giving it a little squeeze.

'Anyway, I should go straight back to La Vieille Maison. I suppose we'll hear more about this affair before long. Don't forget we're meeting tomorrow afternoon.'

'No,' I said, and nodded and went down the steps.

I walked more and more slowly as I approached La Vieille Maison. I was dreading seeing Paul. . . . I was afraid of seeing his face and reading something in it that had not been there before. Yet Paul could *not* have gone into the arena with the intention of shooting Maureille. I just couldn't believe it. There must be many others who would be glad to have the artist dead.

Yet suddenly I was back in that upstairs room at Mas Blandois, hearing Paul's strained voice saying clearly on the breathless summer air:

'Someone will murder you one day, Maureille.'

And then I saw Paul. He was coming from the opposite direction, still carrying the briefcase. He actually smiled and seemed quite pleased to see me.

'Hullo, Damaris! Why, what's the matter? You look— Have you a headache?'

I stared up at him. It was still the face I had seen at lunch; too haggard for so young a man, but certainly not the face of a murderer.

'A – a little. It's very hot. I think I'll lie down for a while.'

'That would be a good idea,' he agreed. 'You aren't used to our summer weather. But it really is hotter than usual. It was like an oven in the office.'

'You've – just been there now?'

'Yes. I just looked in with some work I've been going through at home and I found myself staying for a time, talking.'

In my bemused state I had walked past the garden entrance and now we were approaching by way of the front door. Our side of the street was in shadow and I was glad that the light was not shining full on my face. He had been to the office . . . but I had seen him with my own eyes going into the arena. There was not the slightest doubt that it had been Paul, and—

Well, the briefcase was probably big enough to hold
a gun as well as papers. I was very vague about the
size of guns.

'You really do look unwell,' he said, concerned,
and it was he who called Henriette and told her that
I would like some tea in my room and some aspirin if
any could be found. I didn't like to say that I had
already had coffee; I only wanted to be alone to try
and think. So I avoided going through the courtyards,
where I would have had to face Celia's observant
eyes. I went quickly to my room through the winding ways of the old house, slipped off my dress, put
on a thin housecoat, and flung myself on the
bed. When Henriette herself brought the tea and
the aspirin I was lying there with my eyes
shut.

'I'm all right, thank you,' I said, in answer to her
anxious fussing. 'Just the heat. . . . I'll rest for an
hour, then I'll be fine.'

But 'rest' was hardly the word for that hour of fruit-
less thought. I just didn't know what to do, whether
to tell Paul that I had seen him going into the arena
and ask for an explanation or keep my own painful
counsel. And I was afraid . . . afraid for Paul . . . afraid
for me. For every time I was with him he attracted me
more strongly.

It was Valérien who brought home the news of
what had happened in the arena. He was late that
evening – it was nearly six-thirty – and we were all,
even Paul, in the courtyard. My heart leaped sicken-
ingly as I watched Paul's face, and what I seemed to

read there was at first incredulity and then unmistakable relief. But he *had* looked surprised; I was certain he had looked as surprised as anyone else there. Certainly more so than I, who had not even tried to control my face. But no one was looking at me, they were all looking at Valérien, who was embroidering his news with what facts he had learned.

If Paul had already known that Maureille was dead then he was a good actor, and I didn't really think that he would be. He had control, he could to some extent hide his feelings, but I didn't think he was capable of simulating that first blank, incredulous amazement.

It was apparent, too, during dinner – at least to me – that he was quite incapable of hiding his wild relief now that he knew that Maureille was dead. But I was in the know, and perhaps it wasn't so obvious to everyone else that he was in higher spirits than at any time since I had met him. Yet I did see Celia exchange looks with her aunt, as though questioning the change.

After dinner I walked in the garden, as had grown to be my habit. I loved it in the dark under the brilliant summer stars. Not that it was very dark; the moon was growing quite big and shedding a soft silver light. The wonderful smells, brought out by the great heat of the day, lingered magically everywhere. But nothing else was magic; I was still sunk deeply into my troubled thoughts.

Presently I saw someone flitting along the path towards me and for a moment I thought it must be

Celia. Yet she couldn't flit with that awkward plaster on her leg.

It was Louise, breathless, almost incoherent.

'Mademoiselle, Henriette sent me to warn you . . the police are here. They've come to see M. Paul.'

Instantly I felt sick. The blood pounded in my ears; it really did, though it sounds like a cliché.

'The police! But, Louise, why?'

She was very young. I knew that she had only been working for the Gironelles for a couple of months.

'Something to do with M. Maureille.' Her voice was quivering and she looked very pale in the moonlight. 'I know no more, Mademoiselle.'

Of course she must already have heard about the murder, and clearly the arrival of the police had upset her. It had upset me, too. It was like a nightmare.

I waited until Louise had gone, then I began to hurry as quickly as possible to the door that gave on to my steep stair, praying that it wouldn't yet be locked. I didn't know where the police were, and I didn't want anyone to see me until I had done what must be done. I had to try and find out if Paul had had a gun, and, if so, whether he had hidden it well. Yes, I was so besotted with Paul Gironelle that I was quite prepared to hide evidence of murder. But I didn't *believe* – I never did believe it for one moment – that he had shot Jules Maureille.

Still, I had to make sure. I knew which room was his, for I had seen him coming out of it more than once. It was in the main building.

The door was unlocked and I climbed rapidly,

then snatched up an electric torch from the table beside my bed and walked along passages and up and down steps until I was approaching Paul's room. There was a window in the passage that looked down into the biggest courtyard. The lights were on in the house and the shutters had all been closed to keep out the mosquitoes, but I applied my eye to the small patch of netting that was supposed to let the air come in. The lamps threw pools of light over the courtyard and several people were down there. After a moment I realized that only Paul was missing. No one was talking much; there seemed to be a stunned silence. Then I heard Celia say:

'But what can Paul have had to do with Jules Maureille?'

I went on, praying that none of the servants would catch me. Paul himself was presumably closeted somewhere with the police officers. I slipped into his room without putting on the light; the shutters were closed, but I didn't want to risk light being seen through the netting. I thought it also looked down on the courtyard, so I kept my torch low and partly shaded it with my hand.

It was a very orderly room. There were two big bookcases filled mainly with law books. Great tomes that looked very erudite. I hadn't realized that Paul was so brainy. He had an intelligent face, but he didn't look the scholarly kind. There were magazines on the table by his bed, toilet things on the dressing-table, a pale robe hanging on a hook behind the door. There was no sign of the briefcase, so I was forced to open the wardrobe doors and then the door of the big cupboard. At once, as I peered into the cupboard, my heart leaped, for the briefcase was lying on the middle shelf, looking absolutely innocent, almost flat.

I lifted it out and carried it to the bed, where I could put down the torch so that it would cast a low beam. The briefcase *was* almost empty. There was just one thickish envelope that seemed to hold papers relating to a client, judging by the scrawl on it. There was most certainly no gun, and, when I cautiously applied my nose to the inside of it, no smell but the fragrance of good leather. I was vague about such things, naturally, but it seemed pretty certain that a gun recently fired and put back would smell quite strongly. Of course he could have thrown the gun away at once, perhaps finding a hole for it in those dark passages in the heart of the arena. The police would already have searched there, I was sure.

I put the briefcase back and shut the cupboard. I was convinced now that no gun had returned with Paul to La Vieille Maison. I was certain, really, that no gun had gone out with him, either.

I looked to see that I had left everything as before and then slipped out into the bright light of the corridor. There were male voices coming up the stairs – the ones that went down to the corner near the front door. One voice said sternly:

'—never advisable, Monsieur, to keep blackmail to oneself. Now if you had come to us—'

So they knew about the blackmail! I think I felt sicker then than at any time that day. If they knew *that* they might try to pin the murder on to Paul, even if they did not know that he had actually been in the arena. Perhaps they could produce witnesses to swear that he had been there. I might not have been the only one who had seen him, though I would have said that no one else could possibly have noticed. The Americans had been crowding in front of the ticket booth; the attendants could hardly have noticed when Paul slipped in so quickly. It was just that, to me, that tallish figure in the yellow shirt, with the dark hair and the well-poised neck, was so important, so significant.

I tried to hear more, but it seemed that Paul was showing them out into the street. There was a chorus of *'Bonne nuit, Monsieur!'* It didn't sound as though they had arrested Paul. In fact they certainly hadn't, for I heard him say, as though to himself: *'Dieu!* What a thing to happen!' The words came clearly up the curving staircase.

I couldn't face him then, so I doubled back through the upper corridors, then down the middle stairs and out into the third court. Its beauty had no power to charm me then; I gave it no thought. I felt terribly alone, shut out. Yet the Gironelles would have to tell me; the whole town would probably soon know that the police had been to La Vieille Maison.

Very slowly I walked towards the main courtyard, where everyone was still gathered. Even Henriette was there now (I knew that she regarded herself almost as part of the family), and Paul himself.

Celia saw me, I thought, but no one else took the slightest notice of me. I stood beyond the pools of light, the outsider in that moment of family trouble, family disbelief.

'But why?' M. Gironelle was demanding sternly. 'For the love of *le bon Dieu*, boy, tell us that! Why should the police come here to question you about Maureille's death? You weren't in the arena this afternoon, I gather. Certainly you went to your office and might pass the arena on the way—'

'They don't think I was in the arena,' Paul said. He was very white and taut, and his eyes looked a little wild. 'They'd *like* to think it was I who shot him, but naturally they've no evidence and never will have. I *didn't* shoot him.'

His mother began to cry quietly. She said through her sobs:

'You're a good shot. Perhaps they know that. You won all those prizes for shooting when you were still a boy at school.'

Paul said almost impatiently:

'I haven't a gun now. I haven't had one for years. I doubt if I could hit an elephant at point blank range. One loses one's eye. Whoever shot Maureille did it from quite a distance, from one of those higher openings in the arena, and the bullet went plumb through the back of his neck.'

Mme Gironelle cried louder, and Valérien, speaking for the first time, asked in a strained voice:

'Then why did they come? Is this all part of whatever's been worrying you during the past weeks – almost months? Was it *Maureille*—?'

Paul said on a note of high desperation:

'Oh, all right. You'll have to know now; there's no way out of it. I'm in a jam without having murder pinned on me. The police went straight to his studio, which he had behind the gallery. His brother was in there and said he had just discovered that it had been ransacked. Some papers seemed to have gone, but they found a list of names that had got stuck at the back of a drawer. My name was one of them. He was blackmailing at least a dozen people. That's why the police came to question me.'

CHAPTER EIGHT

Damaris Knows Too Much

I HAD NEVER imagined that M. Gironelle could look so formidable. He had risen and seemed to be towering over his son.

'And you've been paying that scoundrel money without having the sense to ask me for advice or go to the police?'

'I couldn't do anything else but pay him, Father,' Paul said in a voice that suddenly sounded flat and lifeless. 'He had something on me; he knew something that I couldn't have had made public. Remember my profession. A prospective lawyer must be quite blameless.'

'Well, you're certainly not blameless now, my son, at least in the eyes of the police. They know you were being blackmailed . . . they may suspect you of murder. Did you *tell* them why you were being blackmailed?'

'No, I refused. They didn't press the point, though later . . . I don't know. I suppose I may have to tell them. They were more interested in where I had been this afternoon, and I told them in the office. I was there for at least forty minutes.'

Celia spoke then for the first time. She asked:

'And were you there when Maureille died? In the office, I mean.'

'I must have been on my way there,' Paul said. 'I couldn't myself have said what time I arrived. I went slowly, I stopped for a drink (I've told them that, they can verify it). But M. le Brun apparently says he thinks it was about two-fifty when I reached the office. Jules Maureille was shot at two-forty, or a couple of minutes later.'

'And your office isn't more than five minutes' walk from the arena. Maybe six or seven minutes if you walked slowly. Did you have the drink just before you got to the office?'

Paul faced his father, his eyes blazing again. He looked very handsome and very wild indeed. I shall never forget how I felt, watching him. I shall never forget the words that were spoken that evening.

'Are you convinced that I shot that bounder, then?'

'Naturally not. I merely want some assurance that the police aren't going to try and pin it on you.'

'I had the drink soon after I left here,' Paul said more quietly. 'At Jacques's. I didn't note the time at all. I don't consult my watch every few minutes. I walked slowly. I stopped to buy some cigarettes. . . . I stopped again to tell a tourist the way to the Roman theatre. But if I really reached the office at two-fifty then I must have passed the arena by two-forty.'

'You did pass it, then?'

'I passed it. One does. It's the quickest way between here and the office.'

'But you weren't, apparently, in a hurry. No, my son, *I'm* not trying to pin it on you, but I must know how we stand. I must know now for what you were being blackmailed.'

'*Ah, mon Dieu! Mon Dieu!*' Henriette moaned, rocking herself.

Paul said sharply:

'Go away, Henriette. It's a family matter. Already far too public.'

Henriette gave him a stricken look. I was very sorry for her, she appeared so old and shaken.

'Henriette *is* family,' Valérien said brusquely. 'She'll keep it to herself.'

'The police might get it out of her. I still hope it may be unnecessary for it to come out.' Paul's eyes lighted on me at last, standing in the shadows. 'Is that you, Damaris?'

'I'm sorry,' I said in a quivering voice. 'I shouldn't have listened, but I was so worried. . . . I thought you'd seen me. I wasn't meaning to hide. I'm going now. I – I'm terribly sorry about it all.' And I fled to my room, where, almost automatically, because I just had to do something, I put my used film into the special wrapper that the English firm provided for its return. I wasn't sure how many French stamps it would require, so I dropped it into my bag. The post office was down on the Boulevard des Lices, so I could post it when I went to meet Thomas. If I ever did. I could hardly believe that tomorrow would come and that life would be going on more or less normally.

I undressed and showered and then waited around in my pyjamas and housecoat, with my door open to let in any air there might be and also so that I could hear when Celia came to bed. It seemed a long time before I heard voices, and when I peered round the turn of the passage Valérien and his father were just taking her into her room. They had made a 'chair' of their linked hands.

They left one after the other and I crept along to
Celia's room. She called 'Come in!' and when I
entered she was hopping from the bed to the table
she used as a dressing table. She was very white, either
with pain or worry. Possibly with both.

'Can I help?' I asked, and she said:

'You might gather all my things together for me,
will you? How I curse this rotten foot! Thanks. Yes,
the talc and the face cream and what on earth have
I done with my comb? Well, it's been quite an
evening. A nightmare. And we don't seem out of it
yet. Paul *was* near the arena at the important time,
but he hasn't a gun . . . he wouldn't do it, anyway.
It's a fantastic idea. There were other names on that
list. It might have been any single one of them, or
even someone not on the list at all.' Then she looked
at me sharply, pausing in pinning up her hair.
'Damaris, why were you so interested in Maureille?
You were on to it, weren't you? How, when no one
else had a notion?'

I told her about seeing Paul's face and somehow
putting two and two together; and then, after hesitating, about the conversation I had overheard at Mas
Blandois. But I didn't tell her about seeing Paul go
into the arena. I meant, some time, to get up the
courage to tell *him*, for I just had to know what he
would say. It may sound absurd, but it was a knife
turning in my heart to realize that he had lied to his
father and to everyone. I just couldn't let well enough
alone; I would have to tackle him about it. But he
and no one else should know what I had seen. Certainly I would never betray him.

Celia was a good deal more honest and forthcoming with me. When I had left the courtyard Henriette had gone too, and then Paul had told his family just why he had been blackmailed by Jules Maureille. Briefly, he had been driving across a lonely, winding road on the Camargue and he had not seen an old tramp walking in the middle of the road, just beyond a bend. Tottering, he said he had been; he was very old and very drunk.

Paul had swerved, but the offside wheel had caught the old man and he had fallen, striking his head on the stony road. Paul had got out and seen that the man was dead and he had panicked. It had been an accident, but he couldn't face the questioning, the publicity and trouble, and of course the possibility that he might be convicted of manslaughter. He had returned to the car and driven away, and then he had been horrified to see, a few yards up the road, Maureille's car parked amongst the reeds. But Maureille .himself was not in sight and he had thought he had got away with it.

He had not reported the accident and the next day had seen a paragraph in *Le Provençal* about the old man being found dead. It was thought that he might have been hit by a car, but on the other hand he had had a great deal to drink and might merely have fallen and struck his head, being grazed by a car afterwards. The man had been discovered, it was thought, about two hours after his death, by some Spanish tourists. It was a very lonely road and in a bad condition, and he might easily have lain there for much longer.

So went the newspaper report, and Paul, though suffering from twinges of conscience, had relaxed. Then a day or two later he had received a letter from Jules Maureille, in which he said that he had witnessed the accident, knew Paul was to blame and was surprised that so responsible a citizen had not reported the matter to the police at once. He had suggested, in plain terms, that it would now go very much against M. Paul Gironelle if the police were to have their attention directed towards him. An anonymous letter would be the easiest thing in the world to write, and the police could hardly ignore it. If this were not to happen, M. Gironelle might like to let him have five thousand francs as the price of his continuing discretion.

And Paul had paid, not being able to face a breath of scandal. He had known all too well that, if it came to questioning by the police, he would have had to confess. So he had paid, and paid again, getting all the time further into the clutches of a man who obviously enjoyed seeing others squirm.

In a way the story was a relief to me. It was bad enough, but Paul's crime had been an accident, and he had only shown an understandable lack of courage. It was obvious that his good name was desperately important to him. After all the horrors I had been imagining it might really have been worse, though I supposed I must be sorry about the old tramp.

'I've certainly brought you into a nest of trouble,' Celia said ruefully. 'I'm sorry, Damaris. I'm afraid there'll be no outings with Oncle Jean now. He looks worried to death. Everyone is. But do you know –'

she looked at me more happily than she had done so far – 'Val kissed me good night. They brought me up, you know, but Uncle left first. Val stayed for a moment to talk and then he kissed me. He's never kissed me before. Perhaps it was just cousinly affection, but it didn't quite feel like it.'

'He likes you,' I said. 'I've been sure that he does from the first. Do you think perhaps he always thought it would be Paul whom you'd choose, so he wouldn't show his feelings? Paul must have been pretty obviously in love with you, and you seem to have gone about with him—'

'Yes, I did, until it all got too much for me. Oh, I don't know. But Val was different tonight. Perhaps he *has* seen that things aren't very intimate between Paul and me. Perhaps Paul has even told him that I've turned him down. Oh, if I could think— But Paul's the only one who counts at the moment. He *must* be got out of this mess!'

I left her soon afterwards and went to bed. Paul certainly was the only one who counted with me just then. . . . I was haunted by his face and voice, by the danger of his situation. Yet I wished that Celia might be happy.

Amazingly, perhaps, I fell asleep quickly, but I awoke at first light, to the sound of birds. I was very hot and I went to the window for a breath of morning air. And, as before, there was a robed figure down in the little courtyard. Paul, I thought, too worried to sleep, and it would give me a chance to talk to him. Suddenly I *had* to talk to him.

I slipped on my housecoat and thrust my feet into

slippers. Then I ran the comb a couple of times through my hair and padded cautiously from the room, creeping past Celia's door. All the other windows facing the little court were corridor ones, so there was small chance, at that hour, of our being seen or overheard.

Someone always opened the shutters when the lights were turned off and light was seeping in, but the stairs were very dark. The lower door was bolted on the inside, so Paul must have left the house the other way. I shot the bolt as quietly as I could and stepped out through the white porch into the strange luminous light. The chestnut leaves were quite motionless; a few birds twittered. And Paul was standing close to the arch opposite, smoking and staring straight towards me.

'Damaris!' he said, when I was within a couple of feet of him. 'Can't *you* sleep, either? But you have a blameless conscience!'

I looked up into his face. I couldn't see it clearly, for he was in the shadow of the arch.

'I haven't. Paul, I had to speak to you, and when I saw you down here . . . Paul, I saw you go into the arena. I was there, and I was still there when the shot was fired. I saw you slip past the ticket booth and the American party, going in, but I didn't see you after that. When I realized what had happened to Jules Maureille I left quickly, because – because I thought it was best not to chance being questioned. I knew you hated Jules Maureille. I was so frightened—'

He was silent for what seemed a very long time and the cigarette burned in his hand. Then he said:

'It might have been someone else you saw. If I swear to you that I only passed the arena—?'

'Paul, you can't swear. I know it was you. I shan't tell anyone at all, not even Celia, but I have to understand. You didn't go there to – kill him?'

'No, I did not. I tell you, I haven't a gun. And who would plan to shoot someone in front of dozens of pairs of eyes? If I'd wanted to kill him I'd have done it in – a more secluded place.' He didn't know, of course, that I had seen him at Mas Blandois.

'Well, someone *did* shoot him in the arena. And if it was through the back of his neck then it must have been from one of the high openings directly opposite to me. But I was taking a photograph, and the Americans were all talking and making a fuss. Whoever did it could have stood well back, anyway. Paul, why were you there?'

He said in an exasperated voice:

'Not to kill him in any kind of way. It just suddenly occurred to me that he might be there and that I ought to try and talk to him again. He wanted some more money by Thursday and I knew I couldn't get it in time. I owe money right and left as it is. I even borrowed quite a large amount from Valérien, without telling him what it was for. I *did* go into the arena, but it was simply on the spur of the moment – no gun! – and I was only there a few minutes. I looked out and saw Maureille was in the very centre and that it was going to take more courage than I possessed to walk across there and tackle him. So I lingered for a little while, trying to think, and then walked out again, past another big party. I never heard the shot, but then I would be unlikely to do so once I'd stepped out into the street. I don't think anyone saw me. Only you.' His voice, as he said the last two words, held a strange note.

I said quickly, eagerly:

'It's a relief to know. I didn't really believe you could ever have shot him, but when you said you hadn't been there – I won't tell the police or anyone here. They don't even know I was in the arena. The police might not – well—'

'If they knew that I was there it would be another fibre to help send me to the guillotine,' he said grimly. 'I may be ruined now, but at least they can't really pin anything on me. You'd certainly better hold your tongue. You know too much yourself, Damaris.'

'I only want you to be safe,' I told him, and I couldn't keep the emotion out of my voice.

He drew in his breath sharply and suddenly; as he leaned forward, his face was quite clear in the brightening dawn light. Then he kissed me, full on the lips. It was only a brief kiss, and then he turned away.

'Pretty young girls shouldn't trouble themselves with murder. Go back to bed and forget it.'

I went, gathering up my long skirt to climb the stairs. I didn't even try to go softly past Celia's door. Paul had kissed me! I thought I would never forget that moment in the courtyard, yet I knew that the kiss had meant nothing. It had just been a salute to a pretty girl – at *least* he thought me attractive! – and perhaps a seal on my promise of silence.

CHAPTER NINE

A Theft in Avignon

SOON AFTER breakfast on that Tuesday morning I knew that I would have to get away from La Vieille Maison for a few hours. I was sharply conscious (though of course the Gironelles didn't mean me to feel like that) that I didn't belong. They just had no idea that Paul's troubles mattered as much to me as to any of them.

Everyone seemed upset and unlike themselves, and even Louise, when she brought coffee and rolls to Celia and me in the courtyard, looked pink-faced and puffy-eyed.

'What's the matter with Louise?' Celia asked, when Henriette passed through the courtyard.

Henriette threw up her hands. She looked older than she had done before the bad news broke.

'I don't know. The young are always so emotional. She's been sniffling off and on ever since the police came, though goodness knows they didn't bother *her*. Though, now I come to think of it, it was before that, when she overheard M. Valérien telling about the murder. Probably thinks she'll be murdered in her bed one night. She isn't very bright, but she's helpful enough. Oh, well, she'll get over it.'

The front page of *Le Provençal* was given over almost entirely to the news of the murder of Jules

Maureille. There was a picture of the arena, with a cross marking the spot, and a long account of the extraordinary happenings. The news that Maureille had been a blackmailer had been released, but of course no names were given. It simply said that the police were interviewing anyone who had had dealings with the artist, and they had also spent a long time with Justin Maureille, the deceased's brother. Apparently, at the time of the murder, he had been sorting paintings in a storeroom behind the gallery and studio, and he had just slipped out for a drink when news of the murder was brought to him. He strongly denied all knowledge of the fact that his brother had been a blackmailer. He had thought that all the money came from the sale of his brother's paintings, which were doing well. He was reported as being very shocked by the whole affair.

At La Vieille Maison no one seemed to know how to pass the time. I saw M. Gironelle walking backwards and forwards in the garden, his hands behind him and his brow creased with worry. So I slipped out the front way, with my handbag, guide book and camera. I thought I might as well go and see the Alyscamps, or I should turn into a caged lion like the others. Valérien was the lucky one, having to go to the shop. Yet, though it had not been in the paper, the news that the police had visited the Gironelles might have got out and it would be easy for the townspeople to put two and two together. Valérien might have to face questions and thinly veiled curiosity.

I even thought that I was looked at curiously myself as I walked away from La Vieille Maison. At all

events I had no real urge to go sight-seeing, but I had
to do something and it was another heavenly morning, hot already, though it was barely ten o'clock.

It was quite a long walk to the Alyscamps, which
was on the edge of the town. My guide book told me
that it was all that remained of a great necropolis
and had been the ancient approach to Arles via the
Aurelian Way. But I couldn't really take it in; I
could only think of the horrors of the previous day
and of my early morning talk with Paul.

Yet when I came to the entrance of that tree-lined
vista, with the ancient, empty tombs on either side, I
couldn't help but be captured by its atmosphere. The
air was so sweet and fragrant, the sunlight glittered
down through the leaves and there was such complete
peace that it was hard to believe the teeming, noisy
town of Arles was so near.

I wandered along, occasionally looking at tombs,
or trying to identify trees. There were very few
people about, as it was so early. There was a guide,
who had a small party of tourists clustered round him,
but he made no attempt to persuade me to join the
group.

I walked on, enjoying my solitude, for the guide
and party were going the other way, towards the
entrance. The only other person in sight was a small,
very dark man who was ambling along some distance
behind me. He didn't look like a tourist and he didn't
seem to be paying much attention to his surroundings. He looked lost in thought.

I came presently to the end of the avenue, which
was blocked by the partly ruined church of St

Honorat. I wandered round looking at the outside of the building, then I ventured into the very dark interior. There was a great deal more of it than I had supposed, arches and pillars and remote nooks and crannies. Even when I had removed my sun-glasses it still seemed dark and I was suddenly extremely conscious of the silence. It was very eerie there and once more the weight of centuries seemed to oppress me. Yet I wasn't relieved when I heard slow footsteps approaching. Somehow it was vaguely disturbing.

I slipped behind a pillar and waited, and after a few moments the dark man who had been sauntering along appeared. Clearly he was bewildered by the gloom and I took advantage of his rather groping progress to the right to slip away soundlessly on my rubber soles. I couldn't explain this at all. I had no reason whatever for distrusting him. But slip away I did, very relieved to be back in the sunlight and to see the guide approaching with a new party. This time he did try and annex me, smiling very charmingly, but I made an excuse and left, walking much quicker than before.

Being away from La Vieille Maison wasn't really working. I wanted to know if there had been any more developments, so I decided that I would just go and post my film and then return. After all, I would be out that afternoon with Thomas.

At the busy crossroads I turned left into the Boulevard des Lices and soon I was at the post office. A clerk told me the right stamps for the film and I dropped it into the box, then remembered that I could do with some stamps for letters and cards. I was just turning back to the counter when the door opened and the small, dark man strolled in. He didn't glance in my direction, but went to one of the clerks and asked for stamps. He was certainly French, and probably of the south, though the clerk didn't seem to know him.

I wondered why on earth he should have made me uneasy, and, putting away my stamps, set off to walk through the gardens and so back to La Vieille Maison. As I went I tried not to look at the arena, but it is remarkably hard to avoid seeing anything so large as a Roman amphitheatre. Yet it wasn't any good getting nightmares about what had happened in Arles. I still had to see the arena in Nîmes, said to be even finer, and the Roman theatre at Orange. The Pont du Gard too; perhaps Thomas would take me there that afternoon.

Nothing new had happened when I returned to La Vieille Maison. The police had not returned and Paul was talking to Celia, with his long legs outstretched and a glass of wine in his hand. He gave me a casual smile, as though he had never kissed me in the dawn light. Well, of course I had known it meant nothing, but it hurt to have proof of the fact.

I was glad, really, that I was going out with Thomas, who was kind and uncomplicated. One had to have rest from pain and longing and pleasure and fear.

Thomas said that of course we would go to the Pont du Gard and we drove away across country, at first over the northern reaches of the Camargue. I longed to tell Thomas the whole story of what was worrying me, but I knew I must not. So I had to talk in a rather guarded way about the murder in the arena, and he seemed a little puzzled and worried about me.

'Upset you, didn't it? I don't wonder. But it's nothing to do with you, after all, so cheer up.'

'If only you knew, Thomas! If only you knew,' I said to myself. But I was comforted by his cheerfulness and so obvious sanity. This was only our third meeting, but I felt, strangely, that I knew him quite well. And though, of course, it was nothing like looking at Paul, I couldn't help finding a certain pleasure in watching the dashing way he drove the little car. He had nice brown hands and arms, and his shoulders under his thin shirt looked very supple and strong.

We drove through the Provençal countryside, which was drowned in heat and golden summer light. The stubble fields sometimes had a faint sheen and so had the ripening apples in the orchards. The Pont du Gard took my breath away and I even forgot Paul and the murder for a time. The river, the trees, the great golden arches . . . It was stupendous.

Afterwards Thomas said that we would go to Avignon and soon I was seeing the pale bastions and soaring ramparts again. It seemed quite fantastic that it was only Tuesday and nowhere near a week since I stepped off the train with Celia. I seemed to have gone through an age of experience.

Thomas drove us round the outside of the walls and suddenly I gave a cry, for I had caught my first glimpse of the little broken bridge of the song. The bridge of St Bénézet, broken for three hundred years

or more. In spite of the fact that I had expected to dis-
like the song for always after hearing it whistled by
Jules Maureille, I was enchanted and even hummed
a few bars of 'Sur le Pont d'Avignon'.

I was even more enchanted when we stood on the
bridge, with the Rhône flowing swiftly beneath the
arches and Avignon rising on its hill, a jumble of
ancient golden buildings, with the Palace of the
Popes and the Cathedral of Notre Dame des Doms
dominating the lower roofs. At the side of the
Cathedral were trees and high rocks and Thomas said
we'd climb up there, because it was said to be one of
the finest views in Europe and he thought it was probably true.

As we left the bridge, which we had to do by way
of a little house built into the city wall, I jumped and
clutched Thomas's arm for a moment.

'What's the matter?' he asked, looking surprised.

'That man! Over there on the other side of the
road, looking down at the river now. He was in the
Alyscamps this morning, and then in the post office. I
did vaguely wonder if he was following me, but of
course I thought that silly. And now he's *here*!'

'Very ordinary-looking man,' Thomas said reassuringly, but looking still more surprised. 'A
typical Frenchman of a certain kind, I'd have said.
You must be mistaken, Damaris. About being followed, I mean. Though I shouldn't really blame the
chap, and you know what Frenchmen are said to be!
It probably isn't the same man at all.'

Well, I didn't insist, but I was pretty sure. It was
really too hot to walk all the way to the high gardens,

so we got into the car and Thomas drove to the Palace of the Popes, where he managed to park the car in the great square. It was very hot indeed on the exposed steps that led up to the gardens: the breathless, blazing heat of mid-afternoon. The cicadas were making a shrill, strange chirping noise in the trees.

Halfway up I got out my camera and took a picture down the steps and across the frontage of the Palace, then I walked on with the camera in my hand. When we reached the top it was a little more shady and we walked a few steps to an empty seat under a tree. There were only a few people about, mainly in the distance.

But Thomas didn't sit there for long. He jumped up and went towards the edge of the hill.

'Come and look, Damaris! It's superb today. So clear.'

I jumped up and ran to his side. It certainly was superb, for we looked over the Rhône and the little bridge towards Villeneuve on its hill. The hill was crowned by a great golden fort, and below it the tawny roofs of the old town were lovely in the sun. There was a small machine near us that, when one dropped in a coin and pressed the right button, gave a commentary in one of three or four languages. We pressed the French button and stood side by side, still staring at the view and listening to the pleasant voice telling us about what we could see.

It must have been nearly ten minutes before I realized that the camera case hanging on my shoulder was empty. I spun round and darted back to the seat, but the camera was not there.

'Oh, Thomas, my camera!' I cried. 'It was in my hand as we came up the hill, and when we sat down I put it on the seat. I jumped up when you called, forgetting all about it. It's gone!'

Thomas stared at me and then at the seat.

'You've got your bag all right?'

'Yes, it's here. It's always on my arm. But the camera, Thomas—'

He began to wander round, looking at other seats, and he even asked a French family if they had seen anyone pick up a camera. They said they had only been there a minute or two and had not seen anyone come near. They certainly hadn't noticed a camera.

I was very upset about it, because it had been a present and I couldn't afford another as good.

'It was so silly of me to leave it there. But I never thought – I didn't hear anyone.'

'We wouldn't, I suppose, with that commentary going on,' Thomas said, frowning. 'And we had our backs to the seat pretty well all the time. I'm terribly sorry, Damaris.'

Well, the theft spoilt the rest of the outing, but, though I was distressed to lose my camera, I didn't for a moment suspect that it had any special significance.

But the next morning something else happened. I offered to do some shopping for Henriette, but I didn't linger over it. I thought it high time that I wrote a proper letter to my family, though I didn't intend to tell them much – or even anything – about the murder and Paul's involvement with Jules Maureille. They would only worry, and might even

insist that I must join them in Devon. I just couldn't
bear the thought of going away from La Vieille
Maison; to leave Paul . . . not to know what was happening. No, even though life was strained and not
very pleasant, I had to stay there.

I went up to my room to fetch my writing materials
and, as usual, the bed had been made and everything
polished and tidied. It was only when I opened my
drawers in search of my pad, which I had thrust away
somewhere, that I became suspicious. Things were
certainly not as I had left them. They were tidy, too
tidy, and most things had been moved, I was sure of
that. I knew that Louise or the other young girl,
Violette, usually did my room, sometimes, but not
always, supervised by Henriette. Perhaps, unsuper-
vised, one of them had been curious. It need have
been no more than that.

But, rather annoyed, I pulled my cases from under
the bed, and when I opened them they, too, had been
disturbed. I had left quite a lot of odd things in them
that I had thought I wouldn't want immediately. One
recognizes one's own muddle and this was certainly
no disorder of mine. Whoever had gone through my
cases had not taken time to disguise the fact. Perhaps
they had heard someone coming.

My first instinct was to go and find Henriette and
tell her what had happened. She could speak tactfully
to the young things. But then I pushed the cases back
and sat down on the bed with a bump. I don't know
why, but I suddenly connected this searching of my
possessions with the theft of my camera the previous
day. My camera! I had been taking a photograph at

the very moment that the murder took place, and, strangely perhaps, that was the first time it occurred to me that that picture might be important. *Someone* might think it important, but it would have to be someone who knew I had been in the arena, and the only person who knew that was Paul.

Yet if Paul was not the murderer (and I was sure that he was not), then someone else had killed Jules Maureille from a point just across the arena from where I had been. I had snatched up the camera very quickly; perhaps it was only after the shot had been fired that the unknown killer had realized what I had done. But would the killer realize who I was? Wouldn't he have been far more likely to think me a member of that big party that had been milling all around me?

The roll of film had gone to England, since it was one of those that had to be returned to the makers to be developed. But only Thomas knew that I had changed the film immediately after taking that last shot in the arena, and it was even possible that he had not noticed, since he had been busy at the time. Anyone else would probably think that the same film was still in the camera. Colour films held a great many exposures.

Thinking of posting the film the previous morning, I remembered the man who had seemed to follow me. He had arrived in the post office after I had thrust the small package into the box, so *he* wouldn't know. And I was fairly sure – no, I was certain – that he had been in Avignon. He could have followed us up to the Rocher des Doms and quietly taken the camera while we were absorbed in the view. Though I had looked back down the steps and right across the Place du Palais and I had not seen him. There were, however, several cafés opposite the Palace of the Popes. He could have sat at a table and watched us until we were safely out of sight, or even waited in a car. There had been dozens of cars parked in rows and I should never have noticed him.

Then, supposing he had stolen the film, he would have seen very soon that it was a French film and near the beginning of the roll. He would have had it developed, perhaps, to make sure. And the next step would be to try to find the other roll of film. It would probably have been easy enough for someone to make his way unseen through the garden and up my steep stairs, but no outsider could possibly have known where I slept in the big, rambling house.

No, that simply wouldn't hold water. If my theory had any validity at all, someone who knew the house and its workings had searched my room. Paul could have done it, naturally; so could the girls or Gaston or Henriette.

With the beginning of a headache, I tried desperately to think further, but I was hopelessly stuck. I only knew that, though I was rather frightened, I had to keep it to myself for the time being. The only alternative was to tell the whole story, and at all costs I wanted to keep out of the presence of the police. As Paul had said, I knew too much and they would get it out of me.

CHAPTER TEN

Danger in Nîmes

LUNCH WAS a very uncomfortable meal. Paul
was morose and abstracted, scarcely looking at
Celia or me, and I found it almost impossible
to behave naturally. Valérien always lunched near
the shop and M. Gironelle was in Marseilles. Since
that terrible evening when the police had come Mme
Gironelle had never quite regained her usual manner
and she looked dreadful, old and haggard.

Paul had said originally that he was going back to
the office on Wednesday, but he was still at home,
wandering restlessly round the house and courtyards
or else occasionally helping Gaston in the garden.

When Celia and I were alone after the meal she
put out her hand and grasped my wrist.

'What *is* it, Damaris? You might tell me. I know
you at least well enough to realize that you're far from
yourself. I'm sure you're hiding something.'

I stared at her uneasily. I *couldn't* tell Celia yet.
For one thing she would be desperately upset to know
that Paul had lied about being in the arena. It would
be all the worse for her because she was anchored
to the couch that had long since been carried out into
the courtyard, so that she could be really comfortable.
Also I had promised Paul not to tell anyone at La
Vieille Maison.

'Is it any wonder that I'm unlike myself after all that's happened?'

'Yes, I know, but there's something more. Damaris, I've been watching you. . . . I've seen the way you look at Paul. Does he— Are you attracted to him?'

I felt the burning colour flooding all over my face and neck. I couldn't speak and after a few moments she went on contritely:

'That wasn't fair. I'm sorry. But it's true, then? I suppose perhaps it was inevitable. He *is* very attractive and, in a strange way, more so now that he looks so much older and graver. But Damaris—'

'All right,' I said roughly. 'I know he doesn't really know that I exist. But I can't help it. It just happened. I never believed before in love at first sight. Look, I'm sorry to leave you, but Mme Gironelle said she'd sit with you later and get on with her embroidery. I'm going to Nîmes. I have to do something.'

'Good idea! The buses go from the station, I think. Gaston will have a time-table. He's very efficient over transport. Nîmes isn't as romantic as Arles or Avignon – much more industrial – but the arena is very fine.' She looked embarrassed at the mention of the arena, then went on hurriedly: 'Oh, well, just because someone was murdered *here* it doesn't mean that you must shrink from the arena at Nîmes. And there's the Maison Carrée and the Temple of Diana in the Jardin de la Fontaine. Heaps of things you ought to see. What a pity you lost your camera!'

But I didn't want to think of the camera. I only wanted to be doing something . . . anything. So, an hour later, I was sitting in a bus speeding towards Nîmes. It was fun to watch the people and to listen to them, and I cheered up a little. Besides, I did love the Provençal countryside, though there was something vaguely oppressive about it under the unvaryingly blue sky.

When I reached Nîmes, which turned out to be quite a big city and, at first glance at least, not very romantic, I went straight to the Roman arena. I thought I might as well get it over, and, in fact, I was very thrilled with it. The fact that its attic storey still remained, while the one at Arles had gone, made it seem much more perfect. The sun blazed down and only a few people were there.

I had by then grown uneasy about being followed, but there had been no one I recognized on the bus and there was certainly no one in the arena.

Afterwards I strolled up the Boulevard Victor Hugo, looking at the shops and stopping to buy some postcards, until I came to the Maison Carrée, a Roman temple with a pillared frontage, and once more the consciousness of the weight of centuries filled my mind. In Britain we often have Roman remains under our feet, but as a rule we don't have them towering over our heads, as glowing and real as they were nearly two thousand years ago.

After that, as I was very hot, I sat at a café table and ordered a *citron pressé*, and then I decided to find my way to the park, in search of the Temple of Diana. There was a plan in my guide book, so I made my way along the bank of a shining canal and then turned towards some gates I saw at the end of a street.

The gates led me into a secluded area of steep steps and heavy trees, with paths winding at many different levels and rather dilapidated seats here and there. At the lower levels there were a few children playing while their mothers sat and read or chatted with each other, but presently I seemed very much alone. However, I was going in the right direction and I thought I would probably find the Jardin de la Fontaine and the Temple of Diana.

It was hotter than ever out of the shade and the paths were rough and dusty. I presently chose a seat under a tree, which gave me a view over a low wall to crowding roof-tops, and there I began to try – unwillingly – to take up my thoughts where they had left off that morning.

Perhaps I dozed, lulled by the sound of birds and insects; at all events, I was completely taken by surprise when suddenly I found something soft being bound around my mouth and a strong arm pinioning me to the seat. A low, hoarse voice, which I realized later must have been deliberately disguised, whispered in French in my ear:

'Do not scream, Mademoiselle. In any case, you would find it difficult to do so at the moment. If you try it, I warn you that I will strangle you at once.'

I tried to struggle, but it was useless. The seat was very old and sloped backwards and I was thoroughly pinioned. Sharp terror surged up in me, but I tried to keep my head. There were people in the park . . . someone would come along. I could even hear children's voices not far away.

The voice went on, hurriedly:

'I want to know only one thing. What did you do with that film that was in your camera? The film you were using when you took photographs in the arena on Monday afternoon? If you have taken it to a shop in Arles, or sent it back to the makers as one does with some films, then I want to know. I will loosen the scarf for just a few moments while you tell me, but I warn you . . . You speak some French, no doubt?'

My mouth was free, but my tongue felt dry and swollen and at first I couldn't speak. Then I croaked:

'I posted the film to England yesterday morning.'

'But the results will be returned to you in Arles?'

'No, I gave my home address,' I said, with a rising surge of anger. 'So please let me go at once. I'll go straight to the police—'

'It would not avail you, Mademoiselle. They would merely think you grew nervous alone in the park. A young English girl, attractive, so naturally politely followed— Your home address, please.'

And just then, blessedly, the children's voices came much nearer. They were shrieking and laughing and I heard the thud of what seemed to be a ball against a tree. My captor said something under his breath and the arm pinioning me was removed. I felt a blow on the side of my head and heard feet running away down the path.

It was not a heavy blow, just enough to confuse me for a few moments. But when I turned my head sufficiently to look down the path it was empty. The corner was only a few yards away from me, but I was too weak and shaken to rise quickly and run to see if I could catch a glimpse of the receding back.

Besides, the children were there, a boy and a girl, with a big red ball. They stared at me curiously as they went past.

I realized that at least they promised safety, so I rose shakily and followed them. Suddenly I hated the gloom under the trees and the brooding silence that lay over most of the place. I must get out and find safety in crowds. I must have another drink, too, as quickly as possible.

Somehow I got myself back into the heart of the city and there I once more ordered a *citron pressé*. I don't believe I thought at all until it came and the delicious ice-cold fluid touched my dry lips.

It had been a *fantastic* occurrence! Almost unbelievable now that I was sitting, unharmed, on a lively and civilized boulevard. But it *had* happened, and at least it had proved to me that my theories about the film had been correct. But what to do now?

I could go to the police and tell them what had happened, leaving out anything about Paul, but if I did so they would insist on seeing the film. They would certainly get it from the makers in England as soon as possible, and the whole point was that I didn't know what was in those pictures of the arena. I had not seen Paul after those first glimpses at the entrance, but there was just a chance that he was on a picture somewhere. And if he were in the murder picture . . . No, I couldn't risk it. Yet my captor had certainly not been Paul; I had glimpsed his hands and they had not been Paul's, which I would have known anywhere.

The man in the park had either been the murderer

or an accomplice. Would it help if I told that part of
it? Left out all mention of the film and merely said
that I had been in the arena, just opposite to where
the shot had been fired. I could say that the mysterious man in the park had been going to kill me
and then maybe it would lead all suspicion away
from Paul. The man thought I knew something
and . . .

I thought I would go crazy with doubt and in-
decision. I had to tell someone, or I really should go
mad. And Thomas suddenly came into my mind;
Thomas who seemed so safe and sane and who obviously had a good brain. I *knew* I could trust Thomas.
I knew he wouldn't betray any confidences, and he
might give me some much needed advice. He was an
outsider in the whole affair; he would be able to see it
in perspective. And I was meeting Thomas for dinner
that evening.

I felt better when I had come to that much of a
decision and I was suddenly in a hurry to get back
to Arles. It was quite useless to think of doing any
more sight-seeing. I felt safe enough in the heart of
the city, but it was a nasty thought that I must have
been followed all the way from La Vieille Maison. As
I walked to the station and boarded the bus, someone
must have been there. Perhaps he had followed by
car, for unless another stranger was involved in the
affair, I was sure that there had been no one on the
bus I had ever seen before.

I saw myself standing in the arena, then strolling
towards the Maison Carrée. Someone must have
waited outside the arena and then followed me all the

way to the remote seat under the tree. No, I didn't like the thought at all.

I was glad when I was on the bus again, squashed into a window seat by an immense woman with a market basket. I felt safe enough in her garlic-smelling, benevolent presence.

When I returned to La Vieille Maison I found everything as it had been before. The police had not come back, which might or might not be a good sign. Valérien, arriving soon after me, reported that there were endless rumours in the town, and he gathered that the police were being very active. They had interviewed Justin Maureille again and Charles Rondeau, who sometimes helped in the gallery, and apparently a great many other people.

I could hardly wait to get out to meet Thomas, and I was very relieved when I saw him waiting at our usual café. He saw at once that I was very excited, and I promised to tell him just as soon as we were quite alone, probably not until after dinner.

He wisely took the hint and we walked to the Place du Forum and ate at a restaurant there. In spite of everything I was terribly hungry, and while we ate he just made general conversation. But his gaze was often on me, and we didn't linger over our coffee.

'Come on, Damaris. I've got to know. It's something pretty serious, isn't it?'

'It would help if you'd just listen and then tell me exactly what you think,' I said, as we began to stroll south again.

'I'll do that.' And he took my arm in a comforting

grip. But I didn't start the story until we were walking beside the canal that Van Gogh painted. It was
already dark, the velvet, enchanting darkness of
Provence, but there were lights here and there and
the moon was rising. After I had glanced behind us
several times I was pretty sure that no one was following; at any rate they couldn't get near enough to
hear.

'Thomas, I haven't known you long, but I do trust
you,' I began.

'So you should,' he said gently.

'But you must swear that you won't tell another
soul until I give you leave. It's a matter of life and
death.'

If he thought that I was being unnecessarily
dramatic he didn't show it. His hand tightened and
he said gravely:

'Of course I swear. Get on with it, my dear.'

So I told him everything, every single detail, starting with the way Celia had not seemed to want me to
accompany her to Provence. He asked an occasional
question, but mostly he just listened intently. It was
only over Paul that I had any difficulty, but I told
him exactly what had happened, leaving out only
that brief kiss in the courtyard. It was a relief to speak
of the whole incredible affair.

The only real reaction he showed was when I got
to what happened in Nîmes, and then he looked
really horrified.

'My *dear* Damaris! Why on earth did you go wandering alone in a place like that?'

'But I didn't know I was in any danger. And

nothing actually happened to me. The children came in time. I won't be so silly again.'

'I should think not! Stay in crowded places for the present, for heaven's sake.'

'But what am I to do, Thomas? What do you think?'

He paused to light a cigarette, then walked on for some distance in silence.

'It's an extraordinary story,' he said at last. 'You *ought* to tell the whole thing to the police at once, but I see that you feel that you can't because of endangering Paul. Yet, if you did, they might get on to the track of the real murderer.'

'You – you don't believe it was Paul?'

'It doesn't really seem like it. Of course I don't know him, but there seem to be others in it besides Paul Gironelle. It might be any of the other people who were being blackmailed. The police will be watching all of them, of course, but some will have had alibis, and Paul was, they know, at least passing the arena at about the approximate time.' Then he said in quite a different voice: 'You like this Paul, don't you?'

'Yes,' I answered, very low. 'Yes, I do. I *couldn't* cause him any more suffering.'

'Oh, dear!' he said, and his tone was so sad that it startled me. 'Oh, Damaris! I don't want you to be in love with anyone else.'

'But – but, Thomas, we only met on Sunday.'

'And you only met Paul Gironelle on Friday, so there isn't much in it.' Then his voice changed again, becoming brisker. 'Look! I'll have to think about it.

I must try and get it straight. So don't do anything
drastic until we meet again. As it happens, I'm off
tomorrow evening as well, so will you meet me at six,
usual place? And in the meantime play safe. Keep
with other people and watch what you do.'

'All right, Thomas,' I agreed meekly.

'Promise? About keeping with people, I mean.'

'Of course. I was scared to death in Nîmes. I don't
want to be in any more danger.'

After that he walked back with me to the garden
entrance of La Vieille Maison and watched me go inside. I think he was still there when I reached the
garden door and stepped into the second courtyard.

At once I was surprised and uneasy, for the house
blazed with lights. Some of the shutters were still
wide, as though no one had remembered to close
them. And, as I stood there, Henriette came almost
running towards me.

'Oh, Mademoiselle Damaris, the police are here
again! They came with a search warrant after they
received an anonymous letter. They searched M.
Paul's room and have found a gun.'

CHAPTER ELEVEN

Paul Is Accused

I STOOD VERY still, staring at her, and in spite of the hot evening I was suddenly shivering, cold as ice. The old woman looked terrible, as though she had aged ten years since I went out. Her cheeks were sunken and her lips were quivering.

'It isn't true,' I said at last, almost flatly.

'It's true enough,' Henriette said harshly. 'Oh, Mademoiselle, it is the end of the world!'

'But it's a mistake. Of course it must be a mistake. Paul wouldn't kill anyone and he hasn't got a gun.'

'It must certainly be a mistake,' Henriette agreed. 'M. Paul is not the violent kind, even when he is being blackmailed. I have known him since he was a little boy; I know him as well as anyone, Mademoiselle. He didn't kill Jules Maureille. But the police – the thick-headed fools! – believe that he did.'

'But where *was* the gun? Have you heard that?'

'In his big cupboard, in the briefcase he took out that day,' she said. 'And, you see, they have found someone who will swear that they saw him coming out of the arena. They say it was only a very few minutes before all the fuss that arose when the murder was discovered.'

'Oh, dear heaven!' I cried, feeling sick as well as

cold. 'But, Henriette, there's one thing. I – I went to his room and looked in that briefcase on Monday evening when the police were here. The gun wasn't there then.'

A faint look of hope spread slowly over her ravaged face.

'You *looked*? But why?'

'I – I don't know. I didn't think he'd done it, but for some reason I wanted to be sure. There was nothing in the briefcase but an envelope with papers in it. I even sniffed to see if there was a smell of gunpowder.'

'The papers were still there, it seems. M. Paul says he has done no work since Monday; hasn't felt like it. Quite natural, too, if you ask me. Then, Mademoiselle, you'll tell the police?'

'Are they still here? Is – is Paul still here?'

'In the living room. Talking . . . talking . . . Me, I have been listening at the door. That's how I know so much,' Henriette confessed, without shame. 'Oh, I never thought to live to see such tragedy in this family! Everything is falling to pieces. There's Gaston breaking his heart – M. Paul has always been his favourite – and little Louise having hysterics. I sent her to her room to get her out of the way. As for the others – the ones who really matter – go to them, Mademoiselle Damaris. And then for pity's sake tell the police that there was no gun.'

They were all there in the largest courtyard, and certainly that time I had no eyes for the beautiful surroundings in the light of the lamps with the moon floating so brilliantly high overhead. As I walked slowly towards them, moving out of the shadows, it looked like the setting of some tragic play.

Mme Gironelle was crying heart-brokenly, M. Gironelle sat beside her, in stony silence, and Valérien and Celia sat together on the sofa. Valérien was holding her hand, but Celia, white-faced and big-eyed, seemed completely unaware of the fact. As I approached they all turned towards me.

'You've heard?' M. Gironelle asked.

'Henriette has just told me,' I said, and hardly recognized my own voice. 'I – I can't tell you—'

'There's nothing to say, except that, of course, he didn't do it,' said Mme Gironelle thickly, then she collapsed again, burying her face in a white handkerchief.

I sat down – I had to, my legs were shaking so badly – and told them what I had already told Henriette. As they listened I saw faint looks of hope on all the faces except Mme Gironelle's which was still hidden.

'But why did you do that?' M. Gironelle asked, as Henriette had done.

'I – I don't know. I was frightened. I didn't think for a moment that Paul had done it, but – but I *had* to look for a gun.'

I saw Celia flash a glance at me and knew that she, at least, understood something of my state of mind, though of course she knew nothing about my seeing Paul enter the arena.

'It's a thousand blessings that you did,' said M. Gironelle and rose. 'Come, Damaris. We must go and tell this to the police at once.'

I rose, too, but before we could move any more

Paul came out through the glass door. There were two police officers close on his heels. The sight of Paul was almost too much for me; he was ashen, but his head was held very high.

'I have to go,' he said, in quite a strong voice.

'But, my son, do you mean that you are to be arrested?'

'I've been accused of the murder of Jules Maureille,' Paul said steadily.

I moved then. I went forward, passing Paul, until I stood close to the two officers. They were nice-looking men and vaguely I got the impression that they were not enjoying the affair much more than the rest of us. Of course the name of Gironelle stood high in the town.

'You must please listen to me,' I said and I was alarmed at the way my voice shook. I wanted it to sound decisive, so that there could be no doubts about my integrity. 'I – I searched Paul's room on Monday evening when you were here. It was – just a precaution, just to prove beyond doubt that it was – was impossible for him to have murdered Jules Maureille. I never really *thought* he had.' And I flashed a desperate look at Paul, which I realized, too late, that the men had caught. 'I carried that brief-case to the bed and opened it and there was nothing in it but one big envelope full of papers. There was no gun and no smell of gunpowder. It – it must have been planted.' I had to search my mind wildly for the last word. My French could desert me in a crisis.

The two officers exchanged glances. One of them asked politely:

'Mademoiselle reads detective stories?'

'No, I don't. Almost never. But – but it must have been, if it wasn't there on Monday.'

'By whom, Mademoiselle?'

I stared at them helplessly. Yes, by whom? Who, in that house, would wish to make sure that Paul was accused of a murder that he had never committed? I could think of no one, naturally. It was fantastic to dwell on such a thing. But, come to that, who could have sent the anonymous letter that had led the police straight to the gun?

'Someone must have got in from outside,' I said, after a moment. 'It would be quite easy. The doors are always open.'

'And they would know where M. Paul Gironelle slept?'

'They might . . . they might. They could look in other rooms. It wouldn't be impossible.' My voice was growing rather wild.

The senior officer said almost gently:

'Mademoiselle is English?'

'Yes. Yes. What has that to do with it?'

'Nothing, one supposes. Yet the English sometimes do altruistic things. You are perhaps – attached to M. Paul Gironelle?'

The colour flamed and flared in my face. From ice-cold I had gone burning hot all over.

'No. Yes. I mean, we all are, naturally.'

But they were looking at each other again, raising their eyebrows in a slightly sad, understanding way. One took out a notebook and asked for my name and also how long I expected to remain in Provence.

'We will remember your evidence, Mademoiselle. Meanwhile—' And in the terrible silence that followed they took Paul away.

I couldn't stay there in the courtyard. . . . I had to be alone. I rushed away into the shadows, tripping over an old flagstone, nearly falling. Somehow I got myself upstairs, along the corridor and to the blessed solitude of my room. There I flung myself on to the bed and cried more desperately than ever before in my life. For Paul, because he was in such danger and might be lost forever . . . for myself, because I had done my best and been humiliated before them all. For a thousand things, some of them nebulous. I felt I just couldn't bear it.

I don't know how long it was before Celia came to my room. She was walking awkwardly on her cast. She shut the door and groped her way to me in the dark.

'Damaris, don't! Don't cry like that. You'll be ill.'

'I wish I were dead!' I said violently. 'I tried to help and it was no good. I've tried to help all along—'

'Don't you think I feel terrible, too? But we can't die so easily. Probably the case will fall to pieces. . . . Henriette overheard that it's the same make of gun that was used to kill him. It may even be the same gun; they'll find out, of course, when they compare the bullet. But it won't have Paul's finger-prints on it—'

'But how did it *get* there, Celia? Who would do such a thing as to plant it in his room?'

'I don't know,' Celia said shakily. 'It seems an utter mystery. But wouldn't you think that the very fact of its being there would clear Paul, rather than condemn him? No killer would be so f-foolish – so insane – as to leave it there in the briefcase. He would have got rid of it; buried it in a wild part of the garden. Anything. No, there won't be enough evidence.' She went on very unsteadily indeed: 'Damaris, I've known Paul for many years. I don't love him, but he is my cousin, my friend. I – I—' And she burst into tears.

I put my arm round her and we lay there, huddled together, drawing perhaps a little comfort from our shared sorrow and fear.

Presently she went away, but I knew that I wouldn't sleep. I undressed and showered, then put on my pyjamas and housecoat. It was extremely hot, hotter than it had been on any night since my arrival. There seemed to be a brooding, waiting hush, but I supposed it was imagination.

I stood at the window until all the lights went out in the courtyard, then I went softly along the corridor and down the stairs. On the white porch there were a couple of comfortable chairs and I sank into one of them and sat staring out into the silver and black of the little court. I felt that it would be a very long time, if ever, before I could enjoy moonlight again.

I had left my watch upstairs, but occasionally I heard a clock striking in the town. Midnight passed, then one, then two o'clock. The intense quiet was giving place to strange stirrings and sighings, very eerie. It was a little time before my bemused mind realized that the leaves were moving overhead. The wind was getting up, but it seemed no cooler.

When the distant clock struck three I gave up my solitary, pointless vigil and went to bed.

A terrible day followed that decidedly dreadful night. I awoke at eight o'clock to even more blazing light than usual, if that were possible, and to the noise of the wind. The chestnut boughs were thrashing about, shutters were banging. It took me several dazed minutes to realize that this must be the dreaded mistral. Somehow I hadn't understood that it would still be hot when the mistral was blowing. I had always vaguely imagined that it blew from cool grey skies.

A little greyness – the blessed cloudy skies of England – would have been welcome just then. I never thought I should get tired of unvarying sunlight, but that morning my eyes and my head ached and all I really wanted to do was to crawl back into bed as soon as full realization rushed upon me.

Paul had been arrested, he had been accused of the murder of Jules Maureille, and the world – *my* world as well as that of the Gironelles – had come to an end in the courtyard last night.

But I couldn't return to bed and turn my back on life, awful as it was. There might be something I could do, if it was only keeping Celia company during hours that I knew were going to be long.

CHAPTER TWELVE

Damaris Sees Light

THE HOURS *were* long; the day dragged interminably. Henriette went about her duties in grim silence, except when bullying the two young girls, who both seemed completely demoralized. Louise looked like a little, white-faced ghost. But it was the other girl, Violette, who was fetched by a plump and respectable mother about noon. Not much was said, but the whole town knew by then that Paul had been arrested, and clearly a young and innocent girl was not to be left in the guilty household.

Violette was sent to pack her few clothes and ten minutes later the pair departed. Tears were streaming down Violette's pretty face, but it was impossible to know whether she was crying from sorrow or relief.

Mme Gironelle didn't appear until lunch time, and M. Gironelle was away most of the morning, seeing lawyers and the police. Valérien went to the shop rather late, saying that no visitors would realize his connection with the affair (they might not even know anything about the great scandal), and there was no reason why he shouldn't open. 'I must do something!' he said, looking ill and as though he hadn't slept at all.

Before he left he held Celia's hand for a moment and they exchanged a long, troubled look. It seemed to me that without much being said, as far as I knew, those two were growing very intimate. Perhaps it was the one good thing that had come out of the whole awful affair.

My mind baulked almost completely though at all thought of the future. If the totally unbelievable happened and Paul came up for trial and was convicted, how could anyone ever be happy again? Least of all Valérien and Celia, who had been so closely bound to him.

Lunch was a ghastly meal, for M. Gironelle had returned with the news that the gun was the same one that had been used to shoot Jules Maureille. There had been no finger-prints at all on it, but this was probably no help. The police were searching for more evidence, especially for someone who had actually seen Paul in the arena when the shot was fired. A man who lived opposite still swore that he had seen Paul coming out, but Paul himself was insisting that he could only have been seen *passing* the entrance to the arena.

By mid-afternoon I think we were all near breaking point, and the mistral was no help. At the best of times it must be able to drive someone who is perfectly sane and happy to a high pitch of irritation. Gaston was forever tightening the shutters, fastening them back. But one always escaped and bang . . . bang . . . bang it would go, until I could have screamed.

In the sheltered courtyards and garden we were

really out of the wind; it merely raged overhead, and the sun certainly was hot. But if the wind caught one between the shoulder blades it had a totally unexpected cold touch; a knife edge.

Valérien and M. Gironelle were the only ones who went out. I once ventured to the front door and found a small crowd standing out in the narrow street, as though waiting for some further excitement. It was just one more thing to build up the atmosphere of waiting and terror. The other entrance had the big wooden doors folded across and bolted on the inside, after a newspaper reporter had brazenly walked across the garden and found Celia and me in the courtyard.

About four o'clock Thomas telephoned from the Hôtel Romain.

'Are you all right, Damaris? It's a terrible business! I heard about it late last night. Someone came into the hotel and said there was a rumour Gironelle had been arrested.'

'Oh, Thomas!' I was so glad to hear his voice that my not very strong composure was severely shaken. 'Everything is like a nightmare. And he *didn't* do it. I told you, that gun wasn't in his briefcase when I looked on Monday. But the police don't believe me. They think that – well—'

'That you were just trying to save him because you like him? Oh, Damaris! But do come tonight. I have to see you.'

'There are people outside; or there were earlier. It's like a kind of siege.'

'Shall I come for you, then?'

'No, don't,' I said, with more resolution. 'I'll come

to the café. No one will follow *me*. And any danger
I was in will have gone now they've arrested Paul. I'll
be there about six.'

When I had hung up the receiver I went and
peered through the glass panel in the front door. The
watchers seemed to have gone away. Perhaps they
had tired of a long vigil with no excitement at all to
help to pass the time.

I went back and said to Celia:

'Do you think it will be all right if I go out this
evening? I can't help anyone, and – and—'

'Of course,' Celia said. 'I only wish I were more
mobile. Is it Thomas?'

'Yes.'

'You like him, don't you?'

'Oh, yes,' I said carelessly. 'He's sane and nice. But
he's not—' And then my voice faltered. I couldn't
even think of Paul, whom I loved and had suffered
for every minute of the day. 'Will – will the
Gironelles think it unfeeling of me?'

'No, dear. I don't suppose dinner will be a very
pleasant meal. You go and meet your Thomas.'

Now that I had the chance of escape I was eager
to be off. The long hours of pain and inactivity had
taken their toll of me. If there had been anything I
could *do* . . . but there was nothing.

I was ready soon after five-thirty, so I thought I
might take a stroll around the town before meeting
Thomas. I couldn't leave by the garden door, as there
was no one in sight to bolt it after me, so I walked
through the house, and the front door was just
closing softly as I approached it.

I snatched it open again and peered out. There were no sight-seers, but Louise was just walking away up the street. She looked very thin and small, though she wore high heels and always tried to look grown-up when she went out. She had a curiously furtive air, which struck me even in the midst of my own preoccupation.

Just as she reached the corner I stepped quickly into the doorway of a little shop. I hoped I was hidden, but I could still see her, and she looked very carefully behind her.

Louise didn't want to be followed. Why? Was it just the fear of curious townspeople or something more? I left the doorway and walked briskly after her, glad that I had tied a scarf over my hair for, as I came up to the corner, the wind was fierce.

For the first time it was occurring to me that all along Louise had behaved rather strangely, seeming more upset than was quite warranted when she had no connection with the family and had, in fact, only been with the Gironelles for two or three months. Of course very young girls – and perhaps particularly Provençal girls – were apt to be emotional. She could, possibly, think herself in love with Paul. Was that the explanation? Somehow I didn't think it was. She had usually paid more attention to Valérien.

Louise! But she was only about fifteen; an innocent child. Yet she had not looked innocent as she glanced furtively behind her. Well, perhaps she was just going to meet a boy friend and thought

Henriette would try and stop her on that tragic day.

All the same I kept Louise in sight and this was easy, even though the narrow streets were crowded with people: evening strollers who seemed, somehow, to be able to ignore the mistral. She didn't manage the high, thin heels too well and once she seemed to trip. She *still* looked furtive and there was something tense about her thin back.

In the Place du Forum she hesitated and even, for a moment, looked as though she were going to turn back. Then she went on, almost at a run in spite of the heels. She was making for a certain corner . . . she was making for . . . And then the beginning of light penetrated my brain. Louise was making, with nervous haste, straight towards the front entrance of the Galerie Maureille.

I ran too, dashing without apology round the groups of tourists and townsfolk. I came up to the gallery just as Louise burst through the open door. Forgetting caution – I *had* to see and hear – I advanced until I was only a short distance away. And so I heard Justin Maureille, alone in the gallery, say on a high, almost shrill note:

'Louise, you little fool! What are you doing here? Didn't I tell you never to come here? And if you had to, there was the back entrance. For the love of *le bon Dieu* get out of sight!' He was thrusting her through a door as he spoke, but just then he glanced over his shoulder.

I drew back instantly, out of sight of the big window. I didn't know if he had seen me or not. Quite probably not, for his eyes had looked curiously unfocused. But I had been a fool to go so near. Yet I had heard . . .

I was shaking; there was a roaring in my ears. Light was dawning with a vengeance, but it wasn't all clear yet. The mistral whipped my skirt and tossed the ends of my scarf as I went slowly back to the Place du Forum. I had to sit down, anywhere, just for a moment.

I chose a café where the tables were sheltered by a glass partition, but the wind was making the red awning flap. A waiter came to me instantly and I ordered a *citron pressé* that I didn't really want, even though my mouth was dry.

Louise and Justin Maureille! Louise, who had been at La Vieille Maison all the time and had recently been in a rather strange state of nerves. I heard the police officer asking me who could have planted the gun and remembered my blank certainty that no one could have done so. Yet all the time Louise had been connected with Justin Maureille. She could have searched my room for the film and put the gun in Paul's briefcase. Louise, in a hopeless panic, had run to the Galerie Maureille and caused fury and alarm.

But I quite liked the girl. She had seemed a harmless, even a rather charming little thing. That, however, didn't alter the fact that she could have been bullied or blackmailed into doing that terrible thing to Paul.

But if Justin Maureille wanted to make sure that Paul was accused of the murder there must be a reason for it. It was Jules, not Justin, who had hated

Paul, but Jules who had been murdered. And why shouldn't it have been his own brother who murdered him? I was vague about it, but I thought that the facts were supposed to be that he had been sorting canvases behind the gallery and had just gone out for a drink when the news of his brother's death reached him. Well, had the police tried to check if what he said was true? Or had they spent all their time and energy finding that man who had seen Paul? If Paul could get past the ticket booth unobserved by the arena officials, so could someone else. Indeed, they must have. That had been clear to me all along.

Perhaps Justin Maureille had hated his brother; perhaps he had stood to inherit his apparently quite valuable paintings, his money and the ownership of the gallery.

My brain worked furiously and I was suddenly absolutely convinced that I was on the right track. But, glancing at my watch, I saw that it was five minutes to six. I must hurry to meet Thomas and tell him the whole story; then, if he agreed, he could go with me to the police. Once the whole thing was looked into, they were sure to be able to find some connection between Louise and possibly both the Maureilles. Perhaps she was a relative . . . a poor relation from somewhere out of town. I had the impression that she was a country girl – from something Mme Gironelle had said, I thought. And if they looked into Justin Maureille's whereabouts on the afternoon of the murder . . . if they could prove that he had possessed a gun, then the thing might be nearly tied up. If they could get my roll of film from

England perhaps I had even photographed the murderer. I no longer felt much fear that Paul would be in any picture, but, just to be on the safe side, I would keep the existence of the film a secret until some positive evidence had been gathered against Maureille.

I finished my drink and rose. The day that had seemed so endless and dreadful no longer seemed quite so hopeless. Perhaps, after all, I was going to be the one to save Paul.

Disregarding the occasionally cold finger of the mistral, and lost in thought, I walked rapidly away from the Place du Forum to meet Thomas and tell him this new development in the story.

CHAPTER THIRTEEN

A Chase in the Mistral

I WAS RELIEVED, as I approached the café, to see that Thomas was already there, with his car parked at the edge of the pavement. He stood up as I went towards him and said at once:

'Damaris, what is it? Has something else happened? My dear girl—!'

'Yes, something has,' I said breathlessly, but aware that I must be discreet, as the tables near by – those that were out of the wind – were quite crowded. 'Oh, Thomas, I *have* to talk to you!'

'Yes,' he said, accepting the fact without surprise. 'But not here. Let's get out of Arles. I thought we might go to Aigues-Mortes for dinner.'

I knew that Aigues-Mortes was an ancient walled town beyond the Camargue, and originally I had wanted to go there. But now I could only think of what I must soon do.

'I don't think there'll be time for dinner, Thomas. Something has come up. . . . I've seen it all. Or nearly all. I want to talk to you and then we must go to the police.'

'Well, let's drive out somewhere to talk,' Thomas suggested. 'We'll get no privacy in Arles this evening. Everyone is crowding out of the mistral. Damaris, you aren't going to faint?'

'No,' I said hastily, though for a moment I had felt very queer. 'It's just strain and the excitement of the last half-hour. I still can hardly believe it, but I know it's all true. Oh, and the mistral gets on my nerves!'

'It can get on the strongest nerves and yours have had to stand a good deal during the last few days.' He put his hand firmly but gently on my arm and steered me towards the car. 'Come on, Damaris. It's going to be difficult to find any shelter from the wind, but we'll drive out into the Camargue and tuck ourselves into the reeds or some sheltered hollow. I promise I'll drive you straight back if we decide to go to the police.'

'Oh, you are a comfort, Thomas,' I said, and he flushed a little.

'What you really mean is that I'm placid, not like the excitable French.'

'You're a lot more besides.'

I climbed into the car and he went round and got into the driver's seat. The rush hour was in full force, with traffic streaming noisily along the Boulevard des Lices, and it was perhaps the thunder of so many cars and heavy lorries, coupled with the wind, that had affected me so badly.

It was good to cross the Pont de Trinquetaille and head away towards the Camargue. At first we had some of the traffic with us, but most of it turned off and soon we were more or less alone in that vast landscape under the brilliant early evening sky.

Thomas had put the top up, but it flapped in the wind, and I crouched down, glad of the scarf that covered my hair and of the heavy white cardigan I wore. The reeds were bending and swaying . . . the salty pools were a mass of wild ripples.

Thomas drove fast, without talking. Then, when we had covered five or six miles, he said:

'We've got to get out of it somehow before we can talk. What about down here? It looks lower.'

It was the road that led to Mas Blandois.

I nodded and we went that way, and somewhere short of the *mas* he suddenly pulled the car into a grassy hollow. It was a little sheltered, though the mistral roared overhead and made a sharp rustling sound in the reeds.

'We'll be better out of the car,' said Thomas, reaching for an old raincoat that he kept in the back. 'See that little bridge down there? Kind of against it, don't you think?'

'Someone might stand on the bridge and listen,' I said, and he glanced round at what we could see of the landscape and laughed, though without much amusement.

'I don't think so, really. There isn't a soul for miles. You *are* in a state of the jitters! But then it's murder, isn't it? Somehow one side of me just can't believe that you're really involved.'

'I am,' I assured him. 'I certainly am. We mustn't be long. Perhaps we should have stayed in Arles.'

'Back in no time,' he said. He spread the raincoat and saw me settled, then lowered his strong body beside me. It was blessedly sheltered against the little old bridge and even quite hot now that we were out of the wind.

I couldn't relax. I sat bolt upright, hugging my

knees, and once I had started the words poured out of me. I told him all about seeing Louise and the conclusions to which I had come.

'It *must* be right, Thomas. Louise is the connection; there can't be any doubt about it. She must have searched my room and then later put the gun in Paul's briefcase. There *had* to be someone in the house and there's no doubt it was Louise. She's been in such a state; it was very puzzling until I saw her rushing into the Galerie Maureille and then everything came clear. It must have been Maureille who shot his brother, or else that little dark man who was following me. They must be in it together.'

Thomas had also heaved himself bolt upright. I saw clearly and gratefully that he had resigned all hope of a peaceful evening.

'Yes, it must be as you say. The police really ought to know as soon as possible.'

'Oh, Thomas, I thought you might laugh, or at least pour cold water on the whole thing.'

'I don't laugh when I see that something is desperately serious. We'd better get going!'

'But do you think the police will believe me? That's the only thing I'm really afraid of. They didn't before, over the gun.'

'They'll have to take some notice. They may even have had their suspicions of Justin Maureille until they got the anonymous letter about Paul having a gun in his possession. I'm afraid you're right about dinner. When all this is over we'll go to Aigues-Mortes, but not this evening.'

He rose and reached down to take my hand. His

back was to the car and the narrow road, but I was looking that way. Suddenly a car came round the corner and pulled up within a few feet of Thomas's. The driver was Justin Maureille and beside him was the dark man I had seen in the Alyscamps and in Avignon. The man who, almost certainly, had terrorized me in Nîmes.

At first Thomas seemed puzzled by my frozen stare, then he glanced over his shoulder, letting go of my hand. The men were getting out of the car and Justin Maureille was holding a gun.

'It's Maureille!' I croaked. I couldn't really believe it. It seemed like the most fantastic nightmare. 'And – and the other one. They've guessed that I know. . . . He must have seen me when Louise . . . *Thomas!*'

'For heaven's sake!' Thomas cried, looking utterly astonished but not really scared at all. He said later that it had seemed fantastic to him, too.

The men were between us and the car now, and advancing slowly. The other man also had a gun, I saw then, and suddenly, at a word from Justin Maureille, he turned and fired at the front tyres of Thomas's car. The explosions made me jump, but otherwise I seemed frozen to the spot, my back pressed against the sun-warmed stones of the little bridge.

It is very difficult to describe one's reactions when facing a lethal weapon. I had seen plenty of films with much the same situation, but I'd never asked myself what it was like in reality.

The plain truth is that I couldn't believe it. I just could not take in that I might die there on the

Camargue, with the mistral blowing overhead and the reeds a dark line against the evening sky.

I suppose only a few seconds passed, but, looking back, it seems that it could easily have been ten minutes. Then Thomas said in a very low and perfectly steady voice:

'They mean business. There's only one chance. . . . When I give the word throw yourself under the bridge and make for the nearest reeds. Keep as flat as you can and move quickly. I'll do the same.'

The men were still advancing. Maureille said sharply:

'Put your hands up, please. We want to talk to you.'

'Now!' Thomas muttered through the side of his mouth. He had started to raise both hands, but suddenly he made a violent movement with his right one. Something shot with tremendous force towards Maureille, who was in the lead, and he gave a scream of pain. At much the same moment I moved and the gun went off. I dimly knew that the bullet had gone into the side of the bridge within a foot of me, but somehow I had thrown myself sideways and downwards. There was not much water under the bridge, but there was a little.

I crawled rapidly through on my hands and knees . . . not thinking . . . not feeling. Sheer blind panic – but somewhere a grain of sense – made me obey Thomas. The reeds were very near and the way to them lay through a little side channel. I kept my head down, but another shot whistled over me, terrifyingly near.

But I gained the shelter of the reeds, slipping behind a thick bank of them, and found Thomas only a foot or two away from me. Behind us were shouts and a great deal of splashing. The two men were coming after us.

'This way,' Thomas ordered. 'Keep down. Do exactly as I say—'

'We – we can't get through. They'll h-hear!' I gasped.

'They won't hear. The wind is making too much noise and so are they.'

So I obeyed. There was nothing else to do, and long afterwards I thought that Thomas might have had special training for creeping through a particularly difficult piece of country. Reeds – the high, strongly-growing reeds of the Camargue – are just about the most difficult and painful things to find a way through, but find a way he did.

After a few minutes he stopped and signalled to me, and we lay close together in a deep, damp hollow, listening. There were no shots now and at first no sound of movement. The wind, that had been an advantage at first, was adding to our peril then. They might have been very near and we wouldn't necessarily have heard.

Presently Thomas cautiously raised his head, then most of his body. He ducked back immediately.

'Maureille is about fifty yards away. I can't see the other one. Let's go on slowly.'

But suddenly luck wasn't with us. We came to a place where the reeds ended by a marshy pool and our cautious approach alarmed a score or so of birds that had settled for the night. They rose in a noisy cloud and Thomas dragged me back, cursing under his breath. 'That's done it!'

Two more shots came near us and we heard a crashing sound as one of the men approached. Thomas signalled and we began to move the other way, circling the side of the pool and keeping down as much as possible. There were still reeds between us and our pursuers.

By then the whole thing had almost gone beyond the bounds of nightmare. The brilliant westerly light was shining full into my eyes. I felt sick and breathless, and the sweat was pouring down my nose. I still wore my heavy cardigan and it was making me very hot, but it protected me a little from the reeds.

'There's a building!' Thomas murmured suddenly, over his shoulder. 'A *mas*. Not far away, either. If we could make it. . . .'

He went on, quite rapidly, and once I looked up and saw umbrella pines darkly silhouetted and a big whitewashed dwelling. It was only a few hundred yards away.

And then the reeds ended altogether and we were on the edge of drier ground, with no cover whatsoever.

Thomas waited until I reached his side.

'We can lie in the reeds until it gets dark, which won't be long now, or we can make a dash for that place. Once we reach it we're safe. They'd hardly dare to try and get us in front of other people.'

'Thomas, I – I can't make a d-dash!'

But sounds behind us told us that our pursuers had

not given up. They were some little distance away,
but coming on purposefully. And *they* didn't need to
be quiet. They were shouting to each other now.

'You'll have to, Damaris. They'll beat us out otherwise and then we won't have a dog's chance.'

'All right,' I said, as steadily as I could. 'I'll do it.'

'Good girl! It probably is our only chance. Follow
me, but don't run straight. Weave about a little, if
you can. I'm quite a sprinter. How about you?'

'Not b-bad,' I said, remembering the school sports.
But that had been in the calm safety of an English
afternoon.

'O.K. Creep for a few more yards and then put
everything into it. They're still some way off. We may
get out of range pretty quickly. They can't be very
fast themselves.'

Once again I obeyed. I had no doubt that our lives
depended on the next few minutes. Once we reached
the *mas* there would be help . . . maybe a telephone.

We broke cover at almost the same moment and
ran for it. Behind us, after only a few moments, there
were increased shouts and two loud reports. I actually
felt one bullet whistle past my ear. But, miraculously,
terror gave me greater speed than I would have
believed possible. I ran as though fiends were behind
me, as indeed they probably were. And suddenly the
rough ground gave place to a narrow lane that went
straight towards the *mas*.

Eyes staring, panting wildly, I flew after Thomas.
Several more shots were fired, but we had gained a
lot of distance. We were almost up to the big white
dwelling.

'Round to the back!' Thomas shouted. 'That'll be best. There are probably people at the back. I wonder they haven't heard—'

But realization had suddenly dawned on me with sickening force. There were no people. This was Mas Blandois, dark and deserted.

CHAPTER FOURTEEN

A Kind of Haven

'THOMAS!' I GASPED. 'Wait, Thomas!
It's Mas Blandois . . . deserted. The front
door's open. Better get inside.'
He understood at once and came rushing back.
Together we made for the front door. I was slightly
in front then and I pushed the door open and
almost fell inside. Thomas, following on my heels,
banged the door shut behind him and at the same
moment a shattering report and some falling plaster
told us that a bullet had probably gone into the lintel
above the entrance.

It was almost pitch-dark in the big room at first,
but I remembered one thing clearly.

'There's a bar – on the inside,' I panted and groped
frantically for it. My hands closed on smooth, thick
wood and the bar swung easily into place, sinking
down into a kind of socket.

'Good for you!' cried Thomas. His voice echoed in
the rafters above and it sounded amazingly normal.
'But it won't last forever. Empty, is it? Nothing we
can push—?'

And then I remembered what I had scarcely
noticed on my first visit. In a dark corner away from
the fireplace there had been a big wooden table.

'I think there was a table,' I said. 'Over there. I'm
not sure—'

There was. Our groping hands found it. It was

immensely heavy and it took all our strength to move it across the floor. But we rammed one end of it against the door.

'Back door?' Thomas asked briefly.

'I – I don't know. The lower windows are boarded. I never saw a back door.'

It was not quite so dark now. The sunset light was streaming through the exposed tops of the windows. Thomas plunged away into the darkest corner and grunted as he apparently fell down some steps.

'This way, I think. Mind; two steps. Yes, here we are. A good thick door! Were these places built to withstand siege? Bolted and another bar. It would take some breaking down.'

I stumbled to his side and, at his words, the nightmare horror seemed to lessen a little. I gave a small cry and, quite without thinking, flung myself into his arms. They closed round me and I unashamedly shivered and shook, burying my face in his shoulder. I could feel the wild beating of his heart, and his shirt was wet.

'Very nice,' said Thomas, into my hair. 'I only wish you could stay there. But we've got to make sure there are no more doors. Go and stand against a wall, Damaris. They may try shooting through the doors or the boards over the windows. I'll come back.' And he released me and went away. I heard his footsteps echoing as he explored the lower floor.

I leaned my back against the wall, still too shaken even to be ashamed of that moment of weakness. It wasn't Thomas's arms I wished to be in, but Paul's. But there had been something deeply comforting

about that contact with his warm, breathing body
after the terror of the chase.

I remembered that he had been wet, and then for
the first time I realized that I was very damp as well.
The skirt of my dress was soaking and torn and my
sandals were more than sodden. It was a wonder that
I had been able to run so fleetly. Standing there in
the gloom near the back door I gradually became
aware of dozens of small, sharp pains in my legs, arms
and hands and there was one long, burning scratch
on my cheek. A sharp reed, I supposed; it *couldn't*
have been a bullet.

After perhaps two or three minutes my breathing
had quietened and I had assessed what I could feel of
the damage, and it wasn't anything very frightful. I
would live, if Justin Maureille and his friend gave
me the chance to do so.

The silence was suddenly intense. There were no
sounds inside or outside the building. I thought, in a
panic, that Thomas had somehow disappeared, but
just then I found him at my side. I jumped violently
and he gave a faint laugh.

'I took my shoes off. Thought I was advertising my
whereabouts. Better now, Damaris?'

'Yes,' I said firmly. 'Are *you* all right?'

'Scratched and torn and darned damp, but whole
and in my right mind. Where are they, do you think?
Heard anything?'

'Not a thing, since we made all that noise moving
the table. I heard someone outside just before that.
Oh, Thomas, we're safe for the moment. It's a kind
of haven, but—'

He took my hand.

'Let's go upstairs and spy out the land. You said the windows weren't boarded?'

'None of them seemed to be.'

'O.K. Quietly does it. And be careful when we get into any of the rooms. We have gathering darkness on our side, but it's quite light at the moment. Watch it!'

We went softly up the stairs and into the room from which I had overheard the conversation between Paul and Jules Maureille. It seemed a life-time ago. The window looked south and the sunset light stained the whole landscape. About twenty yards away, more or less where Jules Maureille's easel had been, stood the short, dark man, with a gun in his hand. He was directly facing us as we crouched forward, and from where he stood he would command the whole back of the house.

'Hum!' grunted Thomas, and signalled to me to retreat. We repeated the process in a room at the front of the building and there was Justin Maureille in much the same attitude as the other man, commanding the whole front and the side passage between the *mas* and the out-buildings. The brilliant sunset glow lay full across his face and he looked a wild figure, hardly sane. His hair was rising almost straight up from his head and his shirt was half torn off his back, presumably after his passage through the reeds. There was a dark stain all the way down the left side of his face and, as we watched, he mopped at it with the hand that was not holding the gun.

'Got him very nicely, it seems,' said Thomas, with quiet pleasure.

'But what did you do?' I asked, remembering that sudden, unexpected movement of his arm and wrist as we stood by the bridge.

'I'd been playing with a smooth stone just before we got up,' he told me. 'It was still in my right hand, while I was helping you up with my left. I'm a cricketer, a bowler, and I let him have it. First blood to me.' There was definite satisfaction in his voice, and I thought wonderingly that he might almost have been enjoying himself. Men really could be queer.

'But we can't stay here all night!' I heard panic returning to my voice and drew a deep breath.

'Keep calm. We may think up some action. But if we do stay I think we'd be safe enough. I don't believe they'll try and break in.'

'But, Thomas, I'm sure he's mad. He might try anything.'

'He doesn't look too good,' Thomas admitted. He had drawn me right back now, into the upper passage, and he kept his arm round me. 'We're hungry and wet, but it's pretty warm in here. We shan't suffer really.'

It was also remarkably quiet.

'The mistral has stopped,' I whispered.

'It sometimes does at sunset. There's one thing, Damaris. When you don't go home the Gironelles will be worried. They may go to the police.'

'I shouldn't think they'd rush to do that,' I said.

'They'll have to. By midnight, at the latest, they'll be in a real flap. They may think we've had an accident in the car. Did anyone know where you were going?'

'Celia knew I was having dinner with you. I didn't say where. I didn't know.'

'But she knows I've a car? Then that's the first thing they'll think of. The police will look for the car and with luck they'll find it on the road, with bullet holes in the tyres. Then they'll really start looking and this place can't be far from where we parked.'

'No-o. About a mile perhaps, by road. But Thomas, the car's off a very minor road. They might not even think of looking anywhere along it. They'd try the main ones first, to Aigues-Mortes or Les Saintes-Maries. That is, if they started with the Camargue at all. And it's nowhere near midnight yet.'

Thomas peered at his watch.

'Believe it or not, it's not yet eight o'clock.'

And that, in a way, was the most incredible thing of all. So much had happened, and only an hour or two had passed!

'Come and look at the other rooms,' said Thomas, and we continued our cautious exploration. There were windows that looked both east and west, where there were no gunmen standing on guard, and I saw Thomas's thoughtful expression.

'Thomas, we can't!' I cried, in a real panic now. 'We can't make another run for it. We couldn't get round either corner and away, and we would have to go the front way, really. I – I couldn't face any more reeds.'

'Definitely no more reeds,' Thomas said calmly. 'One thing seems rum. Has it struck you?'

'I don't know,' I said. There were plenty of things that seemed to me decidedly 'rum', but I didn't know which of them he meant.

'No shutters on any of the windows. And all these Provençal buildings have them, as a rule.'

'I never thought of that!' I said, surprised. Of course he was right.

I followed him back into one of the westerly rooms, where the glass in the window was broken. He leaned a little way through the gap.

'There have been. Someone must have nicked them, or else the last owners took them away. Well, it's a bit of luck. We'd be worse off if shutters had been closed over every window. They're nearly always noisy things to open.'

'Oh, *Thomas*!'

'Whereas one of these windows would open very quietly – I *hope*.' Then he dragged me back so violently that I stifled a cry. But he was only just in time. The dark man had appeared, walking slowly, with his gun at the ready.

When we were back in the passage he put his arm round me again and held me close to him.

'If they're going to patrol we may well have to spend the night here. By daylight we should really be all right. They can't stay forever and I pin my hopes on someone finding the car – both cars. Damaris *dear*!'

I tried to move away from him.

'Don't, please, Thomas. It's comforting in a way, but—'

'But you don't want to be held by me?'

'I didn't s-say so.'

'Still thinking of Paul Gironelle?'

'I have to think of Paul. He's in prison—'

'And you think yourself in love with him?'

I drew back against the wall and was once more sharply conscious of all my aches and pains. But the worst ache was in my heart.

'I can't help it, Thomas. And if it's any comfort to you, he doesn't even know I exist.'

'It is quite a comfort,' he said grimly. 'But a cold one. Still, time is on my side. We both live in London, after all.'

'When – if – we get out of this it will all seem quite unreal. Away from Provence—'

'The same might apply to you, my girl, and much more possibly.'

'But we can't talk like this. It's silly. Don't you realize just what's happening to us? We're prisoners here, with madmen outside.'

'I realize perfectly, and they're getting impatient, I think.'

Down below there was a thundering knock at the door and a voice shouted:

'Come, please! You English girl and the foolish young man with you! I wish to speak with you.'

'Foolish, am I?' Thomas muttered. We went downstairs and he motioned to me to keep well away from the door. 'The foolish Englishman is here, Maureille. But there's nothing to say.'

'But of course there is. If you will both promise not to go to the police about anything at all we'll let you go safely. On the nearest main road you'll get a lift. You must promise to return to England as soon as possible.'

'It's likely, isn't it? No promises and no safe conduct. You'd shoot us down at once. And how would I explain a car with bullet holes in the tyres?'

'You can do yourselves no good by remaining in there.'

'And no good coming out, either!'

The door began to shake, as Maureille put his whole weight against it, but there seemed no danger on that score. Both the bar and the table were strong. Stronger, surely, even than two men?

We were concentrating on the door, our backs to the windows, and it was more than a shock when suddenly there was a crash of breaking glass. I spun round in time to see a face and an arm in the space at the top of the boards, then there was a flash and a deafening report, followed almost at once by a scrabbling sound, a grunt of pain and the noise of someone falling outside.

But I paid no attention to any of that, beyond registering somewhere in my mind that the dark man had lost an evidently precarious footing. For the ultimate horror had happened. Thomas, without any kind of cry, had crumpled on to the bare floor.

It was very dark where he had fallen and at first I had no idea where he had been shot. I crouched over him crying, 'Thomas! Thomas!' but he didn't answer. I screamed, 'You've killed him, you beasts!' and heard voices outside. Evidently the two men had come together by the front door.

But Thomas was still breathing and my hand touched something warm and sticky on his shoulder.

I moved and could just see that his shirt was already dark with blood. But he certainly wasn't dead.

Something happened to me then that must have been born of sheer desperation. I pulled off my cardigan and wrapped it round him as best I could, knotting the sleeves firmly under his injured shoulder. It was remarkably difficult to do, as he was heavy to lift and my hands were shaking, but it might help to stop the bleeding. Then I stretched him out as comfortably as possible and began to tiptoe towards the stairs. The men were still talking by the door. They seemed to be arguing. I heard one voice say loudly, 'He is dead!'

Perhaps it didn't occur to them that a girl alone could do anything. But I was a girl possessed. I ran softly to the room on the western side. There was still some daylight and in one way the other side of the house would have been safer, but the out-buildings were on the west and if I could reach them that would be something. I opened the window softly. It opened outwards and didn't creak. Then I sat on the sill and paused for just a moment, aware that it was a frighteningly long drop on to hard, sun-baked ground, but I had to do it. I was light and quite a good gymnast. I might get away without spraining an ankle or worse. So I levered myself round and let my body slide over the sill, hanging on by my fingers before dropping.

I landed with a very bad jar, but I scarcely noticed it. In a moment I was up and moving out of sight round the out-buildings. They were very extensive, for they had once housed many horses and perhaps bulls. It was almost dark there and I still had enough sense to realize that someone might have left a bucket or some other object that would make a noise if I tripped over it.

I passed through a very dark passage that smelt faintly of vanished horses and then, as I hesitated, I heard Maureille shouting by the front door. He was telling me that I might as well give up.

But I hadn't given up. The blessed southern dusk was falling rapidly by then, yet if I made for the drive I would be between them and the last light of the sunset. I hated to leave the shelter of the dark pines, but it had to be done. I had to get help for Thomas somehow.

In the end I crawled almost all the way to the road. When I reached it I rose, gasping and sick, and began to run. It was probably nearly two miles to the better road, but I had little hope of finding help before that.

I passed the two cars in the hollow near the bridge. If only I knew how to drive I could perhaps have taken Maureille's car. Maybe he had left the keys. . . . But I *couldn't* drive. I daren't risk trying.

So I stumbled on until at last I dimly saw the corner ahead. When I reached it I stood gasping for breath, praying for something to come along. And when I saw headlights I went as far out into the road as I dared, waving and shouting. But the lorry driver only cursed me in vivid French and waved me back. The heavy vehicle went on its way and silence rolled back over the empty country. Thomas might be bleeding to death at Mas Blandois and I was still miles from Arles.

CHAPTER FIFTEEN

The End of the Story

I DON'T know why, but it never occurred to me to start walking towards Arles, or at least to the nearest house that might have a telephone. I just stood there on the corner, praying for some other vehicle to pass, aware, at the back of my mind, of the Camargue all around me, that ancient area that might be haunted still by galloping, wild white horses. The land was nearly tamed now and people stayed on the ranches simply to have riding holidays, but it hadn't felt tamed that evening and it still didn't as I prayed desperately for something – someone – to come.

And then, probably after only a very few minutes, several police cars came rushing from the direction of Arles. The driver of the first one, seeing me standing there in the headlights, pulled up and shouted to me. I don't know what he said, but I rushed over to the open window.

'Oh, please, I need help at once! Something terrible has happened at the deserted *mas* – Mas Blandois. Thomas is bleeding to death inside and outside two men have guns. One of them is Justin Maureille. I think he murdered his brother.'

Then I knew very little for quite a long time. I was put into the fourth police car, which turned round and drove back to Arles, in spite of my protests that

I had to know what had happened to Thomas. I dimly remember the driver, a kindly man, telling me not to worry. Dimly, too, I gathered that a man from a *mas* further along the road had passed the cars, seen the state of Thomas's tyres and heard shooting over at Mas Blandois. He had gone to the nearest telephone and called the police.

I sat in the front seat beside the driver and shivered uncontrollably, only half conscious, I think. They took me to police headquarters and someone gave me wine, which I didn't want, but I drank a little and felt better. Someone else said, 'I believe the girl is hungry!' and I know I said vaguely that we had had no time for dinner.

Some very good soup was brought to me and I was urged to drink it. I was only halfway through the bowl when M. Gironelle arrived, looking more nearly at the end of his tether than at any time since I had known him, even when they took Paul away.

The soup had already made a difference to me, so I was able to say:

'I'm all right, and I'm sure that Paul will be free now. Justin Maureille murdered his own brother, or got someone else to do it. I know the police will be able to prove it. But oh! I'm so afraid that Thomas is dead!'

It was soon after that that a police officer came to tell us what had happened at Mas Blandois. Justin Maureille had shot himself when he realized that the game was up, but the other man, a man called Victorien Hélot, had been captured. The police had managed to climb into Mas Blandois by the way I had escaped and had found Thomas still unconscious but in no real danger of dying. He was already on his way to hospital.

I suppose the relief of this gave me strength, for when they started to question me I was able to repeat my story quite clearly and concisely, I think. And then they told me that Victorien Hélot had confessed to the murder of Jules Maureille, but he put all the blame on Justin Maureille, who had apparently been no better than his brother, for he had been a blackmailer, too. But they doubted if Hélot would live to come to trial, as he had been shot while resisting capture.

After that everything is very dim indeed. M. Gironelle took me back to La Vieille Maison and it was still not very late, only ten-thirty. They were all in the big courtyard, but it was M. Gironelle who told them most of my story. I suppose I was really the heroine of the hour, for I had saved Paul and the worst of their troubles were over, but I only wanted the peace of my own room.

It was Henriette who tended my cuts and helped me to bed and I remember nothing more until morning, when, at nine o'clock, Paul himself came to wake me.

I stayed on at La Vieille Maison for nearly two more weeks, as we had originally planned. At first I thought that perhaps I had better go home, but the Gironelles insisted that I stay on, and of course my family – still in Devon – knew nothing at all about the tragedy and excitement. The story never reached the English newspapers, for the police did their best to keep me out of it, and there was to be no trial, as Victorien Hélot died three days after the affair at Mas Blandois.

Louise went back to her family, who lived at a small farm near Orange. She had a very bad time with the police, but in the end she was quite free. She was not really wholly to blame for her actions, I suppose, for her family were poor, with many younger children, and when Jules, and later Justin, Maureille offered her money to do certain things she had agreed and only grown frightened when she had to do more than just report on happenings in the household. And of course, when Paul was arrested, she realized just how serious the whole affair was and panicked. Her family was, as I had guessed, distantly related to the Maureilles, and Jules Maureille had made her apply for the job with the Gironelles.

They were strange, bitter-sweet days at La Vieille Maison after Paul came back and the household gradually settled down into a semblance of peace. I shall never forget them, even though they caused me much pain. Paul was there, I saw him every day, and, though he was very charming to me, I knew that soon I would lose him forever. For he was leaving France and going to join his uncle in West Africa, and certainly he didn't love me and never would.

I didn't think he was even in love with Celia any more. He was quiet, remote, almost never gay, and yet just to see him at meals was something. Once he did take Celia and me out in the car and we went to Marseilles and sailed out to Château d'If, a lovely little island in the blue-green bay, with the Mediterranean coast stretching away eastwards. I didn't stay with them; I wandered away and sat on the rocks above the sea, trying, as I was always doing in those days, to come to terms with myself.

I visited Thomas in hospital, of course. The bullet had done no real damage to his shoulder and he was out and back at work in just over a week, but with his arm still in a sling. When I apologized abjectly for leading him into so much trouble he only laughed and said he had quite enjoyed some of it. I told him that Paul was going away and he made almost no comment, for which I was grateful. I liked Thomas more and more as a friend, but I was in no mood to admit to myself that he loved me.

Our last evening came at La Vieille Maison, and we dined as usual under the stars in the big courtyard. I could hardly believe that soon it would only be a memory. I could hardly bear the thought that, by the next evening, I would have to live with the knowledge that I would never see Paul again.

It seemed to be generally accepted by everyone that Celia and Valérien belonged together, but they had not announced their engagement. Celia told me that they were waiting until she returned at Christmas and they planned to be married at Easter. They thought it better to wait until Paul had gone away, though she, like me, was sure that Paul had got over loving her.

After dinner Celia and Valérien went off somewhere in the car and I walked in the garden for the last time. There was no moon now, but the stars were brilliant. Oh, my lovely southern garden that I might never see again! And yet I supposed that, some day, Celia might ask me to stay with them.

While I was still there I heard footsteps on the path that led from the courtyards and there was Paul. He came right up to me and took my hand.

'I never really thanked you for all you did, Damaris. I shall never forget.' And then he kissed me for the second time, and I accepted the kiss as I knew it was meant, though I thought I wouldn't be able to bear the ache in my heart. 'Good-bye, Damaris. You're so pretty. You'll soon find someone else. I'm not the man for you.'

And then he had gone and I stumbled up my dark stair. So he knew! I felt some shame certainly, because I had been rejected, or perhaps never considered, yet in a way I was glad that he had been that much aware of me. At eighteen the pangs of unrequited love are very dreadful, but I think that somewhere in my mind I knew that he was right.

All this happened a year ago, and yet I still remember vividly so much that was said, so much that I felt.

I have a good office job in the City and Thomas has just finished college. We got engaged last week, but we won't be married until the spring. It took me a long time to realize that I loved Thomas, but now I am quite sure of it. Perhaps I never did love Paul; maybe it was only a romantic attachment, born of all those strange circumstances under the southern sun.

Paul is doing very well in Africa, I believe. Celia often writes to me and tells me all the family news.

She and Valérien are living at La Vieille Maison, but the oldest part, where I slept, has been cut off from the main house and they have it to themselves. She sounds very, very happy and in a letter I received this morning she tells me that she is expecting a baby in January. She has asked me to go and spend Christmas with them, but I don't know whether I shall accept. Some day I'll return to Provence, but I think I would rather wait until next summer, when perhaps Thomas and I may go together. Thomas may even take a job in Paris; he has had a very good one offered to him.

A year ago! I have just spread out my photographs and I am looking first at those I took in the early days at La Vieille Maison; the fatal roll of film that caused me so much trouble. The ones of the arena do not show Paul and the murder picture didn't come out. It was the last one on the roll and is nothing but a blur. In a way that seems the final irony.

There are the pictures of Mas Blandois and of course of La Vieille Maison and the beautiful court-yards in sunlight and shadow. Then there is one of Paul standing under a plane tree.

It all happened in Arles and in some ways I now feel a different girl. Yet there are times when a smell or a few bars of music bring back that other, younger Damaris. But I have no fears that my love for Thomas could be shaken by a return to the place where I met Paul. Thomas and I are going to be very happy.